Christmas 1989
THIS BOOK
BELONGS TO:

TO:
JennaZerwas

FROM:
Aunt Angel &
Uncle John

A Child's Book of Stories from Many Lands

CHILDREN'S CLASSICS

This unique series of Children's Classics™ features accessible and highly readable texts paired with the work of talented and brilliant illustrators of bygone days to create fine editions for today's parents and children to rediscover and treasure. Besides being a handsome addition to any home library, this series features genuine bonded-leather spines stamped in gold, full-color illustrations, and high-quality acid-free paper that will enable these books to be passed from one generation to the next.

A Child's Book of Stories from Many Lands

Compiled by
ADA M. SKINNER
and **ELEANOR L. SKINNER**

Illustrated in Color by
JESSIE WILLCOX SMITH

CHILDREN'S CLASSICS
NEW YORK

Portions of this book were previously published under the title
A Child's Book of Modern Stories.

Copyright © 1988 by dilithium Press, Ltd., Children's Classics Division.
All rights reserved.

This 1988 edition is published by Children's Classics, a division of dilithium
Press, Ltd., distributed by Crown Publishers, Inc., 225 Park Avenue South,
New York, New York 10003.

DILITHIUM is a registered trademark and CHILDREN'S CLASSICS is a
trademark of dilithium Press, Ltd.

Printed and bound in the United States of America

Library of Congress Cataloging-in-Publication Data

A Child's book of stories from many lands/compiled by Ada M. Skinner and
    Eleanor L. Skinner; with pictures by Jessie Willcox Smith.
        p.   cm.
    Summary: A collection of stories arranged under the themes "Home
    Tales," "The Story Garden," "Cheerful Stories," and "Tales and Legends
    Beautiful."
    ISBN 0–517–67128–X
    1. Children's stories.   [1. Short Stories.]   I. Skinner, Ada M. (Ada
Maria), b. 1878.   II. Skinner, Eleanor L. (Eleanor Louise), b. 1872.
III. Smith, Jessie Willcox, 1863–1935, ill.
PZ5.C44 1988
[E]—dc19
                                                              88–11840
                                                                  CIP
                                                                   AC

h g f e d c b a

Cover design by Jesse Cohen

CONTENTS

CONTENTS

COLOR ILLUSTRATIONS

Facing Page

PREFACE TO THIS ILLUSTRATED EDITION

IN THIS bouquet of familiar and lesser-known tales from around the world, Jessie Willcox Smith has once more proven her mastery at portraying children in a variety of settings, with affection, artistry, and refreshing realism.

Readers familiar with her illustrations for *A Child's Book of Stories* and *A Little Child's Book of Stories,* two earlier collections in the Children's Classics series, will be delighted to find again her irresistible children in domestic and outdoor scenes— knitting, wading, picking flowers, reading in a hammock, at the beach, or watching goldfish—and generally having a wonderful time of it, as will her readers.

CLAIRE BOOSS
1988   Series Editor

FOREWORD

IT WAS young Mary—and not her kitty—who ate the custard pie. Mary's tearful confession is met with loving hugs from her mother who had known it from the start but "... had hoped that her little daughter would be brave enough to tell her all about it herself." With this simple, pleasing story of a young child's dilemma and its happy resolution, little people and their parents begin a journey—a journey that will take us all to such faraway places as a bewitched cottage in the woods, and deep inside a haystack where magical dwarfs reside. And yet it is not always necessary to travel far—we can visit a backyard garden where little Betty learns to plant and water her own vegetables, or perhaps venture no farther than the antique chair of which Kenneth's parents are so fond, and in which Kenneth loves to sit after a busy day of outdoor play.

Editors Ada M. Skinner and Eleanor L. Skinner, working in the early part of this century, compiled a collection of stories that would serve not only to entertain, but would also instruct children in proper behavior and values. Tales about industriousness, kindness, and perseverance are abundant here, and if these lessons seem too simple or overly familiar, they can be understood as the product of an earlier era. Indeed, it is the old-fashioned quality of these stories, their guilelessness, which makes them such refreshing fare for both the young and the young at heart.

FOREWORD

In the first of four sections comprising *A Child's Book of Stories from Many Lands*, entitled "Home Tales," are stories set in the one surrounding most familiar and comforting to a child—the family home. After meeting the young Kenneth, who imagines conversing with the carved eagles on his father's favorite chair; the convalescing Lucy, snug in her bed with hot soup and ice cream; and other children sharing thoughts and feelings much like their own, young people will come away with a sense of security and well-being. It seems certain that this self-esteem and confidence so effortlessly created by these tales is crucial to a young person's development, for it fosters a child's ability and willingness to seek out experiences and challenges outside the family. Whether by chance or by design, the narratives included in "Home Tales" provide that serenity we hope all children experience and retain.

In "The Story Garden," the young reader or listener is ready to venture beyond the doorstep. Children will follow Betty to her vegetable patch or down the lane to visit the dandelions. Soon they will eavesdrop on the garden tools—Rake, Hoe, and Trowel—each boasting that it is the only indispensable implement (until, of course, they realize that each makes a necessary contribution to the garden's cultivation).

The tales in "The Story Garden" take for their motif the everyday objects, plants, and animals that the young child can regard with the most rapt fascination. Whether these things take on human voices—as do the temperamental little hoptoad and the imperious white butterfly who will not be contradicted—or are simply presented as they are in life, they fill a child

FOREWORD

with wonder while at the same time introducing the world outside in a reassuring way.

The pastoral quality embodied in the first half of this
volume gives way to delightful fairy tale worlds. While the
earlier stories entertained children with tales set in familiar sur-
roundings, the narratives in "Cheerful Stories" and "Tales and
Legends Beautiful" ask the child to enter more fully into realms
experienced in the mind's eye. This type of imaginary land-
scape where there are few landmarks pointing toward one's own
front door is important to a child's growth. These charming
tales not only delight, but also encourage creative thinking—
and creativity, to be sure, is a skill to be coveted, one that
helps us to meet successfully life's many challenges.

These enchanting stories range from the comic to the poig-
nant. On the lighter side is "The Traveling Musicians," the
well-known tale about four old, unloved, and discarded farm
animals who set out to the city to make their fortunes as musicians. Instead, their cacophony of hisses, brays, howls, and
screeches (aided by a dark night sky) scares a skittish band of
robbers from their well-stocked and newly "haunted" hideout.
The traveling musicians are rewarded and need go no further to
enjoy their remaining days. As is true throughout this collection, there are lessons to be learned. The elderly are to be
respected for their past accomplishments and their present
capabilities, and appearances (not only in the dark) can be
deceiving!

Unlike "The Traveling Musicians," "The Banyan Deer" is a
solemn story of honor and ethics. In order to satisfy a king's

FOREWORD

love of hunting, each day a deer is killed—the victim chosen by lots among the deer themselves. A new mother slated to be felled by a cruel arrow begs an audience with the king of the Banyan deer herd. For the sake of her young child, who would not survive without her nurturing, she asks to be spared for a while longer. The Banyan king agrees, and although exempted from this lottery by his human counterpart, takes her place. The greedy king, upon seeing the Banyan leader present himself for sacrifice, is so humbled by this act of supreme selflessness, that he at once frees all the deer and proclaims his forests to be a safe haven for all animals. These disparate tales aptly demonstrate the wide variety of narratives to be both enjoyed and talked about by child and parent.

A Child's Book of Stories from Many Lands creates an atmosphere that radiates warmth, and the luminous color illustrations by the renowned Jessie Willcox Smith perfectly complement the tone of this collection. Her soft colors, velvety lines, and quiet scenes of children in repose or caught in a candid moment of work or play make this treasure trove of children's stories as beckoning and as comforting as a parent's lap.

LEE SANTINI
Editor

New York City
1988

INTRODUCTION

The story is a fascinating type of literature. It offers not only wholesome entertainment to children, but also large means of valuable instruction and training. The merry old nursery jingle cultivates the ear in rhythmic appreciation and stimulates a sense of humour for the grotesque. The exquisite nature myths quicken the child's fancy and attract his attention to the loveliness of the world. Fortunate indeed was the story-teller of long ago who first conceived the immortal tale of "The Three Little Pigs." He delighted his tiny listeners with a simple and interesting plot and at the same time instilled into their hearts the precious lesson of stability and thrift.

To the treasury of old-time stories have been added many valuable tales by modern writers for children. These story-tellers have expressed in artistic form some of life's common incidents and have glorified them by a touch of fancy. The present volume, for the most part, is a collection of such stories. They appeal strongly to the child of today because they picture familiar events which are easily understood. By relating stories which broaden and enrich the child's experience the modern story-teller has contributed a valuable opportunity for training the child to take his place in the social life of today.

EDITORIAL NOTE

THE modern reader may be surprised to discover old-fashioned styles of punctuation and spelling, but these have been retained in order to convey the flavor of the original work.

Home Tales

MARY'S CONFESSION

SHE sat up in bed. The curtain was drawn up, and she saw the moon, and it looked as if it were laughing at her.

"You need not look at me, Moon," she said. "You don't know about it; you can't see in the daytime, Besides, I am going to sleep."

She lay down and tried to go to sleep. Her clock on the mantel went "tick-tock, tick-tock." She generally liked to hear it, but to-night it sounded just as if it said, "I know, I know, I know."

"You don't know, either," said Mary, opening her eyes wide. "You weren't there, you old thing; you were upstairs."

Then Mary tried to go to sleep again. But there was a big lump in her throat. "Oh, I wish I hadn't."

Pretty soon pussy jumped up on the bed, kissed Mary's cheek, and then began to "pur-r-r-r, pur-r-r-r." It was very queer, but that, too, sounded as if pussy said, "I know, I know."

"Yes, you do know, Kitty," said Mary, and then she threw her arms around kitty's neck and cried bitterly. "And—I guess —I want—to—see—my—mamma!"

Mamma opened her arms when she saw the little weeping girl coming, and then Mary told her story.

"I was awfully naughty, Mamma, but I did want the custard pie so bad, and so I ate it up, 'most a whole pie, and then—I—I—oh, I don't want to tell, but I 'spect I must—I shut kitty in the pantry to make you think she did it. But I'm sorry, Mamma."

Then Mamma told Mary that she had known all about it, but she had hoped that the little daughter would be brave enough to tell her all about it herself.

"But, Mamma," she asked, "how did you know it wasn't kitty?"

"Because kitty would never have left a spoon in the pie," replied Mamma, smiling.

THE STRANGER CHILD

IN A cottage which stood near the edge of a thick wood lived a poor laborer with his wife and little children, Karl and Marie. The father worked for his living by felling the forest trees, and although he worked patiently each day for many hours, he was able to earn but a scanty living.

One Christmas Eve the little family gathered around the table and, after the woodcutter thanked God for food and shelter, they began their humble meal.

"This has been a bitter cold day, Father," said the wife.

"It has, indeed," he answered. "I was obliged to stop work early because the snowdrifts piled so high in the forest."

"How cosy and warm we are," said little Marie. "And how quiet it seems when the wind stops howling through the trees."

They finished the evening meal and drew their chairs close about the log fire.

"A story before we go to bed, Father," said Karl. "It's to be about the three wise men who carried gifts to the Christ-child."

"So it is," said Father. "That's the best story I know for Christmas Eve."

"Hark," whispered Marie. "What was that?"

"It's the east wind blowing the fine snow against the window panes," answered Mother. "No one could make his way to the cottage on such a wild night."

5

"I hear it again," said Karl.

"May I come in?" called a small childish voice. "I'm so hungry and tired and I've nowhere to go. Please let me come in."

Marie and Karl sprang to the door and opened it. There, shivering in the storm, stood a little boy.

"Come in!" cried the children.

The little wanderer stepped into the cottage. A gust of wind swept the snow half-way across the room before Karl could close the door.

"Come and warm yourself, little one, and you shall have something to eat," said the mother, drawing the stranger child close to the hearth. "How thinly you are clad."

The father stirred the fire and threw on another log, while little Marie fetched bread from the cupboard.

"Stay with us to-night," whispered Karl who stood very near the wanderer.

"He may have our bed, Mother," said Marie.

"Yes, dear," said the mother. "It is late and I'm sure our little friend is tired. He shall rest here to-night, and perhaps he will tell us his story in the morning."

After the child had eaten the bread and was thoroughly warmed by the glowing fire he was snugly tucked up in the children's bed. A comfortable place for Karl and Marie was made on the wide bench near the fireplace. It was not long before all in the cottage were asleep.

After midnight the snowstorm ceased and the stars shone bright in a clear sky.

THE STRANGER CHILD

"Karl, Karl," whispered Marie. "Wake up! Wake up and hear the music."

Karl sat up in bed and listened.

"Where is it?" he asked.

"Over there, near the window," said Marie. "Isn't it wonderful!"

To the ears of the astonished children floated the sweetest music they had ever heard. Angelic voices, accompanied by silvery-toned harps, were singing:

"O, holy child
With wondrous love!
Our harps we bring
Thy praise to sing.

"O, holy child
With wondrous love!
In peace now sleep
While watch we keep.

"O, holy child
With wondrous love!
The place is blest
Where thou dost rest."

Trembling with joy Karl and Marie slipped out of bed and ran to the window. In the rosy light of the dawn stood a band of angelic children singing. They were dressed in shining robes and each held a golden harp or lute.

For a moment the cottage children stood rapt in wonder at the beautiful vision. A slight noise in the room attracted their attention and turning around they saw the stranger child standing near them. A radiant light shone around his head and in the softest voice he spoke.

"I am the Christ-child. Through the world I wander to bring joy and happiness to little children. You sheltered me and fed me. Behold, I bring joy and blessing."

Then He stepped outside the cottage and stood before the band of angels. He broke a twig from a fir tree which grew near the door and planted it in the ground.

"This twig shall grow into a tree and bear fruit for you each year at Christmastide," He said.

With these words the choristers and the Christ-child vanished; and a marvellous thing happened. Before the eyes of the cottage children the twig grew into a beautiful Christmas tree covered with fruit and nuts. And each year, says the legend, the fir tree which the Christ-child planted bore Christmas fruit and nuts for Karl and Marie.

CHARLOTTE AND THE LITTLE HELPERS

CHARLOTTE was a little girl who lived with her four brothers and two sisters in a little house in a wood. Her mother was dead and her father was too poor to afford help in the home; so Charlotte had to keep her father's house in order and help him with the work on the farm. She was often very tired, for the other children were small and could be of little service to her.

One day, as she sat before the fire mending a dress for one of her sisters, she exclaimed, "Oh, I have so much to do that I cannot work fast enough! If only I had four hands instead of two! Why are not the good fairies on earth any more to help poor children out of their troubles? I wish one could hear me and come to my help."

"Your wish is granted, child. I am here," said a voice, and there, beside Charlotte, stood an old woman. She did not look at all like a fairy, for she wore a long cloak which seemed to cover her from head to foot, and she carried a large basket on her arm.

"Charlotte," she continued in a low voice, "I am sure you are an industrious child. I will help you. See what I have here." And she set the basket on the floor.

"Come," she called; and out of that large basket sprang ten little dwarfs of different sizes. "Here are ten little servants for you, Charlotte. Look at them. The first two are very strong, although rather clumsy and awkward. They will help you to do

9

the heavy work. The next two are taller and more skilled little fellows. The next two are the tallest of all. One is so clever in the use of the needle that he sometimes wears a little cap called a thimble. Here are two others less clever, who often wear fine belts of gold around them. They do very little work alone but they have the last two, which are the littlest, always to help them. Now you will see how industrious these ten little servants can be."

At a word from the old woman five of the little dwarfs began to sew on the dress Charlotte was mending and the other five began to make bread. Charlotte watched them do the heavy work as easily as they did the light work. Surprised and delighted when all was done, the little girl stretched out her arms and begged, "Oh, good fairy, lend me these little creatures and I will ask nothing more."

"I will do better than that, dear child. I will *give* them to you. But to save you the trouble of carrying them about with you, I will make them so small that each one can hide in one of your fingers. Take your places, dwarfs!" called out the old woman; and immediately the ten little fellows hid themselves in Charlotte's fingers.

"Now that you have a servant in each finger," continued the old woman, "you can work much faster than before. But remember that everything depends upon how you treat them. You must keep them always busy—never let them be still. Then the work which has been such a burden to you will be done as if by magic." And with these words the old woman took her basket, opened the door, and went away.

The next morning Charlotte was up very early. She soon

found that she could work twice as fast as before, which made her so happy that she laughed and sang all day long.

"Charlotte," said her father one day, "you are certainly very industrious. No child in the land can work so well or so quickly as you."

Charlotte thought, "Dear father cannot see that I have ten good little servants in my fingers to help me."

AMELIA AND THE DWARFS

ONCE upon a time there lived a couple of gentlefolk who had an only child, a daughter, whose name was Amelia. This little girl had a strong will and a clever head of her own, though she was but a child. She had a way of her own, too, and had it very completely. Perhaps because she was an only child, or perhaps because they were so easy-going, her parents spoiled her. She was, beyond question, the most tiresome little girl in that or in any other neighborhood. From her baby days her father and mother had taken every opportunity of showing her to their friends, and there was not a friend who did not dread the infliction. When the good lady visited her acquaintances she always took Amelia with her, and if the acquaintances were fortunate enough to see from the windows who was coming, they used to snatch up any delicate knick-knacks, or brittle ornaments lying about, and put them away.

If she was not a favourite in the drawing-room, she was still less so in the nursery, where, besides all the hardships naturally belonging to attendance on a spoilt child, the poor nurse was kept, as she said, "on the continual go" by Amelia's reckless destruction of her clothes. It was not fair wear and tear, but it was constant, wilful destruction, which nurse had to repair as best she could.

Amelia's meals were another source of trouble. She would

12

not wear a pinafore; if it had been put on she would burst the strings, and perhaps in throwing it away would knock her plate of mutton broth over the tablecloth and her own dress. The nurse would say, "Many a poor child would thank God for what you waste every meal time, Miss Amelia."

One summer afternoon, during haytime, Amelia had been constantly in the hayfield, and the haymakers had constantly wished that she had been anywhere else. She mislaid the rakes, nearly killed herself and several other persons with a pitchfork, and overturned one haycock after another as fast as they were made. At tea time it was hoped that she would depart, but she teased her mamma to have the tea brought into the field, and so it was brought out.

After this she fell off the haycart, and was a good deal shaken, but not hurt. So she was taken indoors, and the haymakers worked hard and cleared the field, all but a few cocks which were left till the morning.

The sun set, the dew fell, the moon rose. It was a lovely night. Amelia peeped from behind the blinds of the drawing-room windows, and saw four haycocks, each with a deep shadow reposing at its side. The rest of the field was swept clean, and looked pale in the moonshine. It was a lovely night.

"I want to go out," said Amelia. "They will take away those cocks before I can get at them in the morning, and there will be no more jumping and tumbling. I shall go out and have some fun now."

"My dear Amelia, you must not," said her mamma; and her papa added, "I won't hear of it." So Amelia went upstairs to grumble to nurse; but nurse only said, "Now, my dear Miss Amelia, do go quietly to bed, like a dear love. The field is all wet with dew. Besides, it's a moonlight night, and who knows what's abroad? You might see the fairies—bless us—and what not. There's been a magpie hopping up and down near the house all day, and that's a sign of ill luck."

"I don't care for magpies," said Amelia; "I threw a stone at that one to-day."

And she left the nursery and swung downstairs on the rail of the banisters. But she did not go into the drawing-room; she opened the front door and went out into the moonshine.

It was a lovely night. But there was something strange about it. Everything looked asleep, and yet seemed not only awake but watching. There was not a sound, and yet the air seemed full of half sounds. The child was quite alone, and yet at every step she fancied some one behind her, on one side of her, somewhere, and found it only a rustling leaf or a passing shadow. She was soon in the hayfield, where it was just the same; so that when she fancied that something green was moving near the first haycock she thought very little of it, till, coming closer, she plainly perceived by the moonlight a tiny man dressed in green, with a tall, pointed hat, and very, very long tips to his shoes, tying his shoestring with his foot on a stubble stalk. He had the most wizened of faces, and when he got angry with his shoe, he pulled so wry a face that it was quite laughable. At last he stood up, stepping carefully over the stubble, went up to the first haycock, and drawing out a hollow grass stalk blew upon it till his cheeks were puffed like footballs. And yet there was no sound, only a half-sound, as of a horn blown in the far distance, or in a dream. Presently the point of a tall hat, and finally just such another little weazened face poked out through the side of the haycock.

"Can we hold revel here to-night?" asked the little green man.

"That indeed you cannot," answered the other; "we have hardly room to turn round as it is, with all Amelia's dirty frocks."

"Ah!" said the dwarf; and he walked on to the next haycock, Amelia cautiously following.

Here he blew again, and a head was put out as before; on which he said:

"Can we hold revel here to-night?"

"How is it possible?" was the reply, "when there is not a place where one can so much as set down an acorn cup, for Amelia's broken bits of food."

"Fie! fie!" said the dwarf, and went on to the third, where all happened as before; and he asked the old question:

"Can we hold revel here to-night?"

"Can you dance on glass and crockery shreds?" inquired the other. "Amelia's broken gimcracks are everywhere."

"Pshaw!" snorted the dwarf, frowning terribly; and when he came to the fourth haycock he blew such an angry blast that the grass stalk split into seven pieces. But he met with no better success than before. Only the point of a hat came through the hay, and a feeble voice piped in tones of depression: "The broken threads would entangle our feet. It's all Amelia's fault. If we could only get hold of her!"

"If she's wise, she'll keep as far from these haycocks as she can," snarled the dwarf, angrily; and he shook his fist as much as to say, "If she did come, I should not receive her very pleasantly."

Now with Amelia, to hear that she had better not do something, was to make her wish at once to do it; and as she was not at all wanting in courage, she pulled the dwarf's little cloak. "Why shouldn't I come to the haycocks if I want to? They belong to my papa, and I shall come if I like. But you have no business here."

"Nightshade and hemlock!" said the little man, "you are not lacking in impudence. Perhaps Your Sauciness is not quite aware how things are distributed in this world?" saying which he lifted his pointed shoes and began to dance and sing:

> "All under the sun belongs to men,
> And all under the moon to the fairies.
> So, so, so! Ho, ho, ho!
> All under the moon to the fairies."

As he sang, "Ho, ho, ho!" the little man turned head over heels; and though by this time Amelia would gladly have gone away, she could not, for the dwarf seemed to dance and tumble round her, and always to cut off the chance of escape; whilst numberless voices from all around seemed to join in the chorus, with—

> "So, so, so! Ho, ho, ho!
> All under the moon to the fairies."

"And now," said the little man, "to work! And you have plenty of work before you, so trip on, to the first haycock."

Home Tales

Page 1

Charlotte and the Little Helpers

Page 9

"I sha'n't!" said Amelia.

"On with you!" repeated the dwarf.

"I won't!" said Amelia.

But the little man, who was behind her, laid hold of her arm roughly with his lean fingers; so Amelia ran on, and tried to get away. But when she went too fast, the dwarf trod on her heels with his long-pointed shoe, and if she did not go fast enough, he laid hold on her arm roughly and pushed her forward. So for once in her life she was obliged to do as she was told. As they ran, tall hats and wizened faces were popped out on all sides of the haycocks, and whenever the dwarf pushed Amelia, or trod on her heels, they cried, "Ho, ho, ho!"

"Here is Amelia!" shouted the dwarf when they reached the first haycock.

"Ho, ho, ho!" laughed all the others, as they poked out here and there from the hay.

When Amelia saw them she began to shriek for help; but she was pushed into the haycock, where her loudest cries sounded like the chirruping of a grasshopper.

It was really a fine sight to see inside of the haycock.

Farmers do not like to see flowers in a hayfield, but the fairies do. They had arranged all the buttercups in patterns on the haywalls; bunches of meadow-sweet swung from the roof like censers, and perfumed the air; and the ox-eye daisies which formed the ceiling gave a light like stars. But Amelia cared for none of this. She only struggled to peep through the hay.

"Rub her eyes," said the dwarf, "and send her below." On

which Amelia's eyes were rubbed with some ointment, the field opened, and Amelia was pushed underground.

She found herself on a sort of open heath, where no houses were to be seen. Of course there was no moonshine, and yet it was neither daylight nor dark. A light as the light of early dawn was there, and every sound was at once clear and dreamy, like the first sounds of the day coming through the fresh air before sunrise. Beautiful flowers crept over the heath, whose tints were constantly changing in the subdued light; and as the hues changed and blended, the flowers gave forth different perfumes. All would have been charming but that at every few paces the paths were blocked by large clothes-baskets full of soiled frocks. And the frocks were Amelia's. Torn, draggled, wet, covered with sand, mud, and dirt of all kinds, Amelia recognized them.

"You've got to wash them all," said the dwarf, who was behind her as usual; "that's what you've come down for. So the sooner you begin the better."

"I can't," said Amelia; "send them up to nurse, and she'll do them. It is her work."

"What nurse can do she has done, and now it's time for you to begin," said the dwarf. "Sooner or later the mischief done by spoilt children's wilful disobedience comes back on their own hands. Up to a certain point we help them, for we love children, and we are wilful ourselves. But there are limits to everything. If you can't wash your soiled frocks, it is time you learnt to do so, if only that you may know what the trouble is you impose on other people. *She* will teach you."

The dwarf pointed with his long toe to a woman who sat by a

18

fire made upon the heath, where a pot was suspended from crossed poles. It was like a bit of a gypsy encampment, and the woman seemed to be a real woman, not a fairy—which was the case, as Amelia afterwards found. She was the dwarfs' servant.

And this was how it came about that Amelia had to wash her soiled frocks. Let any little girl try to wash one of her dresses; not to half wash it, not to leave it stained with dirty water, but to wash it quite clean. Let her then try to starch and iron it—in short, to make it look as if it had come from the laundress—and she will have some idea of what poor Amelia had to learn to do. There was no help for it. When she was working she very seldom saw the dwarfs; but if she were idle or stubborn, or had any hopes of getting away, one was sure to start up at her elbow and torment her till she did her best. Her back ached with stooping over the wash-tub. Whatever she did not know how to do, the woman of the heath taught her. At first, whilst Amelia was sulky, the woman of the heath was sharp and cross; but when Amelia became willing and obedient, she was good-natured, and even helped her.

The first time that Amelia felt hungry she asked for some food.

"By all means," said one of the dwarfs; "there is plenty down here which belongs to you;" and he led her away till they came to a place like the first, except that it was covered with plates of broken meats; all the bits of good meat, pie, pudding, bread and butter, that Amelia had wasted beforetime.

"I can't eat cold scraps like these," said Amelia, turning away.

"Then what did you ask for food for before you were hungry?" screamed the dwarf, and he sent her about her business.

After a while she became so famished that she was glad to beg humbly to be allowed to go for food; and she ate a cold chop and the remains of a rice pudding with thankfulness. How delicious they tasted! She was surprised herself at the good things she had rejected. After a time she fancied she would like to warm up some of the cold meat in a pan, which the woman of the heath used to cook her own dinner in, and she asked for leave to do so.

"You may do anything you like to make yourself comfortable, if you do it yourself," said she; and Amelia, who had been watching her for many times, became quite expert in cooking up the scraps.

As there was no real daylight underground, so also there was no night. When the old woman was tired she lay down and had a nap, and when she thought that Amelia had earned a rest, she allowed her to do the same. It was never cold, and it never rained, so they slept on the heath among the flowers.

They say that "It's a long lane that has no turning," and the hardest tasks come to an end some time, and Amelia's dresses were clean at last; but then a more wearisome work was before her. They had to be mended. Amelia looked at the jagged rents made by the hedges: the great gaping holes in front where she had put her foot through; the torn tucks and gathers. First she wept, then she bitterly regretted that she had so often refused to do her sewing at home that she was very awkward with her needle. Whether she ever would have got through this task alone is doubtful, but she had by this time become so well-behaved and willing that the old woman was kind to her, and, pitying her blundering attempts, she helped her a great deal; whilst Amelia would cook the old woman's victuals, or repeat stories and pieces of poetry to amuse her.

"How glad I am that I ever learned anything!" thought the poor child; "everything one learns seems to come in useful some time."

At last the dresses were finished.

"Do you think I shall be allowed to go home now?" Amelia asked of the woman of the heath.

"Not yet," said she; "you have got to mend the broken gim-cracks next."

"But when I have done all my tasks," Amelia said; "will they let me go then?"

"That depends," said the woman. "You see, when you first came you were such a peevish, selfish, wilful, useless, and ill-mannered little miss, that neither the fairies nor anybody else were likely to keep you any longer than necessary. But now you are such a willing, handy, and civil little thing, and so pretty and graceful withal, that I think it is very likely that they will want to keep you altogether. I think you had better make up your mind to it. They are kindly little folk, and will make a pet of you in the end."

"Oh, no, no!" moaned poor Amelia; "I want to be with my mother, my poor dear mother! I want to make up for being a bad child so long."

"I will give you some advice. Can you dance?" asked the old woman.

"Yes," said Amelia; "I did learn to dance pretty well."

"During any spare moments you find," continued the woman, "dance, dance all your dances, and as well as you can. The dwarfs love dancing."

"And then?" said Amelia.

"Then, perhaps some night they will take you up to dance with them in the meadows above ground."

"But I could not get away. They would tread on my heels—oh! I could never escape them."

"I know that," said the woman; "your only chance is this. If ever, when dancing in the meadows, you can find a four-leaved clover, hold it in your hand and wish to be at home. Then no one can stop you. Meanwhile, I advise you to seem happy, that they may think you are content, and have forgotten the world. And dance, above all, dance!"

And Amelia, not to be behindhand, began then and there to dance some pretty figures on the heath. As she was dancing the dwarf came by.

"Ho, ho!" said he, "you can dance, can you?"

"When I am happy, I can," said Amelia, performing several graceful movements as she spoke.

"What are you pleased about now?" snapped the dwarf, suspiciously.

"Have I not reason?" said Amelia. "The dresses are washed and mended."

"Then up with them!" returned the dwarf. On which half a dozen elves popped the whole lot into a big basket and kicked them up into the world, where they found their way to the right wardrobes somehow.

As the woman of the heath had said, Amelia was soon set to a new task. When she bade the old woman farewell, she asked if she could do something to help her if ever she was allowed her liberty.

"Can I not help you get back to your old home?" Amelia cried, for she thought of others now as well as herself.

"No, thank you," returned the old woman; "I am used to this, and do not care to return. I have been here a long time—how long I do not know; for as there is neither daylight nor dark we have no measure of time—long, I am sure, very long. The light and noise up yonder would now be too much for me. But I wish you well, and, above all, remember to dance!"

The new scene of Amelia's labours was a more rocky part of the heath, where grey granite boulders served for seats and tables, and sometimes for workshops and anvils, as in one place, where a grotesque and grimy old dwarf sat forging rivets to mend china and glass. A fire in a hollow of the boulder served for a forge, and on the flatter part was his anvil. The rocks were covered in all directions with the knick-knacks and ornaments that Amelia had at various times destroyed.

"If you please, sir," she said to the dwarf, "I am Amelia." The dwarf left off blowing at his forge and looked at her.

"Then I wonder you're not ashamed of yourself," said he.

"I am ashamed of myself," said poor Amelia, "very much ashamed. I should like to mend these things if I can."

"Well, you can't say more than that," said the dwarf, in a mollified tone, for he was a kindly little creature; "bring that china bowl here, and I'll show you how to set to work."

AMELIA AND THE DWARFS

Poor Amelia did not get on very fast, but she tried her best. As to the dwarf, it was truly wonderful to see how he worked. Things seemed to mend themselves at his touch, and he was so proud of his skill, and so particular, that he generally did over again the things which Amelia had done after her fashion. The first time he gave her a few minutes in which to rest and amuse herself, she held out her little skirt, and began one of her prettiest dances.

"Rivets and trivets!" shrieked the little man, "How you dance! It is charming! I say it is charming! On with you! Fa, la fa! La, fa la! It gives me the fidgets in my shoe points to see you!" and forthwith down he jumped, and began capering about.

"I am a good dancer myself," said the little man. "Do you know the 'Hop, Skip, and a Jump' dance?"

"I do not think I do," said Amelia.

"It is much admired," said the dwarf, "when I dance it;" and he thereupon tucked up the little leather apron in which he worked, and performed some curious antics on one leg.

"That is the Hop," he observed, pausing for a moment. "The Skip is thus. You throw out your left leg as high and as far as you can, and as you drop on the toe of your left foot you fling out the right leg in the same manner, and so on. This is the Jump," with which he turned a somersault and disappeared from view. When Amelia next saw him he was sitting cross-legged on his boulder.

"Good, wasn't it?" he said.

"Wonderful!" Amelia replied.

"Now it's your turn again," said the dwarf.

But Amelia cunningly replied: "I'm afraid I must go on with my work."

"Pshaw!" said the little tinker. "Give me your work. I can do more in a minute than you in a month, and better to boot. Now dance again."

"Do you know this?" said Amelia, and she danced a few paces of a polka mazurka.

"Admirable!" cried the little man. "Stay"—and he drew an old violin from behind the rock; "now dance again, and mark the time well, so that I may catch the measure, and then I will accompany you."

Which accordingly he did, improvising a very spirited tune, which had, however, the peculiar subdued and weird effect of all the other sounds in this strange region.

"The fiddle came from up yonder," said the little man. "It was smashed to atoms in the world and thrown away. But ho, ho, ho! There is nothing that I cannot mend, and a mended fiddle is an amended fiddle. It improves the tone. Now teach me that dance, and I will patch up all the rest of the gimcracks. Is it a bargain?"

"By all means," said Amelia; and she began to explain the dance to the best of her ability.

"Charming! charming!" cried the dwarf. "We have no such dance ourselves. We only dance hand in hand, and round and round, when we dance together. Now I will learn the step, and then I will put my arm round your waist and dance with you."

Amelia looked at the dwarf. He was very smutty, and old, and weazened. Truly, a queer partner! But "handsome is that handsome does;" and he had done her a good turn. So when he had learned the step, he put his arm round Amelia's waist, and they danced together. His shoe points were very much in the way, but otherwise he danced very well.

Then he set to work on the broken ornaments, and they were all very soon "as good as new." But they were not kicked up into the world, for, as the dwarfs said, they would be sure to break on the road. So they kept them and used them.

"Have I any other tasks?" Amelia inquired.

"One more," said the dwarfs; and she was led farther on to a smooth mossy green, thickly covered with what looked like bits of broken thread. One would think it had been a milliner's work-room from the first invention of needles and thread.

"What are these?" Amelia asked.

"They are the broken threads of all the conversations you have interrupted," was the reply; "and pretty dangerous work it is to dance here now, with threads getting round one's shoe points. Dance a hornpipe in a herring-net, and you'll know what it is!"

Amelia began to pick up the threads, but it was tedious work. She had cleared a yard or two, and her back was aching terribly, when she heard the fiddle and the mazurka behind her; and look-ing round she saw the old dwarf, who was playing away, and making the most hideous grimaces as his chin pressed the violin.

"Dance, my lady, dance!" he shouted.

"I do not think I can," said Amelia; "I am so weary with stooping over my work."

"Then rest a few minutes," he answered, "and I will play you a jig. A jig is a beautiful dance, such life, such spirit! So!"

And he played faster and faster, his arm, his face, his fiddle-bow all seemed working together; and as he played, the threads danced themselves into three heaps.

"That is not bad, is it?" said the dwarf; "and now for our own dance," and he played the mazurka. "Get the measure well into your head. Lâ, la fă lâ! Lâ, la fă lâ! So!"

And throwing away his fiddle, he caught Amelia round the waist, and they danced as before. After which, she had no difficulty in putting the three heaps of thread into a basket.

"Where are these to be kicked to?" asked the young goblins.

"To the four winds of heaven," said the old dwarf.

Thus Amelia's tasks were ended; but not a word was said of her return home. The dwarfs were now very kind, and made so much of her that it was evident that they meant her to remain with them. Amelia often cooked for them, and she danced and played with them, and never showed a sign of discontent; but her heart ached for home, and when she was alone she would bury her face in the flowers and cry for her mother.

One day she overheard the dwarfs in consultation.

"The moon is full to-morrow," said one—("Then I have been a month down here," thought Amelia; "it was full moon that night")—"shall we dance in the Mary Meads?"

"By all means," said the old tinker dwarf; "and we will take Amelia, and dance my dance."

"Is it safe?" said another.

"Look how content she is," said the old dwarf, "and, oh! how she dances; my feet tickle at the bare thought."

"The ordinary run of mortals do not see us," continued the

objector; "but she is visible to anyone. And there are men and women who wander in the moonlight, and the Mary Meads are near her old home."

"I will make her a hat of touchwood," said the old dwarf, "so that even if she is seen it will look like a will-o'-the-wisp bobbing up and down. If she does not come, I will not. I must dance my dance. You do not know what it is! We two alone move together with a grace which even here is remarkable. But when I think that up yonder we shall have attendant shadows echoing our movements, I long for the moment to arrive."

"So be it," said the others; and Amelia wore the touchwood hat, and went up with them to the Mary Meads.

Amelia and the dwarf danced the mazurka, and their shadows, now as short as themselves, then long and gigantic, danced beside them. As the moon went down, and the shadows lengthened, the dwarf was in raptures.

As for poor Amelia, she found no four-leaved clover, and at cockcrow they all went underground.

"We will dance on Hunch Hill to-morrow," said the dwarfs.

All went as before; not a clover plant of any kind did Amelia see, and at cockcrow the revel broke up.

On the following night they danced in the hayfield. The old stubble was now almost hidden by green clover. There was a grand fairy dance—a round dance, which does not mean, as with us, a dance for two partners, but a dance where all join hands and dance round and round in a circle with appropriate antics. Round they went, faster and faster, the pointed shoes now meeting in the center like the spokes of a wheel, now kicked out behind like spikes, and then scamper, caper, hurry! They seemed to fly, when suddenly the ring broke at one corner, and nothing being stronger than its weakest point, the whole circle was sent flying over the field.

"Ho, ho, ho!" laughed the dwarfs, for they are good-humoured little folk and do not mind a tumble.

"Ha, ha, ha," laughed Amelia, for she had fallen with her fingers on a four-leaved clover.

She put it behind her back, for the old tinker dwarf was coming up to her, wiping the mud from his face with his leathern apron.

"Now for our dance!" he shrieked. "And I have made up my mind—partners now and partners always. You are incomparable. For three hundred years I have not met with your equal."

But Amelia held the four-leaved clover above her head, and cried from her very heart, "I want to go home!"

The dwarf gave a yell of disappointment, and at this instant Amelia found herself in bed in her own home.

"Mamma, mamma! Mother, my dear, dear mother!"

The tender, humble, loving tone of voice was so unlike Amelia's old imperious snarl, that her mother hardly recognized it. "I hope you will never suffer any more from my wilfulness," said Amelia.

Amelia made several attempts to relate her adventures, but she found that neither her mother nor the nurse would believe in them.

"Why, you told me yourself I might meet with the fairies," said Amelia, reproachfully.

"So I did, my dear," nurse replied, "and they say that it's that put it into your head. And I'm sure what you say about the dwarfs and all is as good as a printed book, though you can't think that ever I would have let any dirty clothes store up like that, let alone your frocks, my dear. Well, to be sure, as you say, if you'd been washing and working for a month in a place without a bit of sun, or a bed to lie on, and scraps to eat, it would be enough to do it; and many's the poor child that has to, and gets worn and old before her time. But, my dear, whatever you think, give in to your mother; you'll never repent giving in to your mother, my dear, the longest day you live."

So, in spite of the past, Amelia grew up unselfish and considerate for others. She was unusually clever, as those who have been with the "Little People" are said always to be.

And she became so popular with her mother's acquaintances that they said: "We will no longer call her Amelia, for it was a name we learned to dislike, but we will call her Amy, that is to say, 'Beloved.' "

THE OLD WOMAN
AND THE POT OF DAFFODILS

"A LITTLE girl named Laura," said daddy, "had been quite
ill. One day she was wondering if she would ever feel like herself again, able to do things and to play around. She was sitting up by the window in a big chair. She was looking out,
feeling very sad and forlorn, when suddenly she saw a funny
old woman who looked just like a witch stop by the window
and then walk right into the room.

"The funny old woman spoke at once.

"'Don't be frightened,' she said. 'I'm not going to hurt
you. Instead, you see this pot of daffodils I am carrying?'

"'Yes,' exclaimed Laura. 'Aren't they beautiful?'

"'I am so glad you like them,' continued the old woman,
'for they are for you.'

"'For me?' repeated Laura. 'For me?'

"'Yes,' said the old woman. 'When the spring comes I take
a walk each day, carrying with me a pot of daffodils. When I
see some one sitting in the window of a house looking sick and
longing to go out I just go right in and leave my pot of
daffodils, for they are better than any spring tonic, to my
mind.'

THE OLD WOMAN AND THE POT OF DAFFODILS

"And the yellow flowers smiled at Laura and bobbed their pretty heads, saying, 'We'll make you well.'

"And, sure enough, they really did more toward making Laura well than anything else. How could she help but feel better with the bright flowers smiling at her and cheering her up?"

THE SQUIRRELS' SPRING WORK

"A LITTLE girl named Gwen had fixed a squirrel house on a pear tree near an old apple tree," said daddy. "Now, the apple tree was near Gwen's bedroom, and the squirrels could jump from the apple tree to her window-sill, where they were very likely to find nuts waiting for them.

"When the days began to get a little warmer Gwen hung just outside the window-sill a little hammock and waited to see if the squirrels would dare to swing in it. Having all the nuts Gwen put on her window-sill and seeing her do such kind things so often made them pretty tame. And, too, they appeared to realize that it was Gwen who had seen to the building of the little house.

"But the hammock seemed very strange to them at first. However, one very brave squirrel thought he'd try it and jumped into the hammock. Gwen was watching back of a curtain, and it was all she could do to keep from crying aloud with joy, for she was so pleased that one of the squirrels was actually using her little hammock. After a while the other squirrels tried it.

"Before long one of the old squirrels began to scold for all he was worth. Oh, he was very much annoyed, and all the squirrels stopped swinging in the hammock. They seemed to be paying great attention to the old squirrel, and Gwen wondered what it was all about.

"The old squirrel was the leader, and he was the one who always gave the directions and did all the managing. This, in squirrel language, was what he said:

"'Now, don't you know you can't spend your time idling! You are the laziest lot of squirrels I have ever known. Don't you know that you must get to work? This is the season for us to tap the syrup from maple trees, and you are spending your time swinging in a hammock. It is all very well to play, but then there is work to be done. We don't want to waste our time and let all the good sap go, do we? And you really do want the maple syrup, don't you?'

"Off they started to scamper to the nearest maple tree. Gwen put on her hat and coat and followed along to see what they were going to do. They got all the sap they wanted and smacked their lips over it. They enjoyed the work really, for it meant good times to follow, and they were glad the wise old squirrel had told them about it in plenty of time."

LUCY'S VISITORS

Lucy had been sick in bed with a sore throat for several days, but finally she woke up in the morning to find that the sore throat was almost all gone. You can imagine her delight to find the nice visitors that came to see her that same day.

A most attractive little toy wooden bunny came. His ears could be moved up and down and a most roguish look he would have when one ear was up and the other down.

Lucy gave him chicken broth and he was extremely pleased.

If he had not been afraid his wooden face would have cracked he would surely have smiled. For it was pleasant indeed when one was only a little wooden bunny rabbit to be given chicken broth.

It was most superior chicken broth, too. Oh, yes, for it had been made for Lucy and was made so as to give her lots of extra strength.

Besides the toy bunny a rag doll came to see Lucy. Yes, a very lovable sweet rag doll came to visit her.

She wore a little knitted hood on her head and a little sweater and a knitted scarf to keep her warm.

And she had a pair of warm knitted shoes. She wore her

outside jacket, too, over her sweater, and she took along her little apron, so she could wear that when she played, so as not to hurt her good dress.

Oh, yes, the rag doll was going to play with Lucy and have an excellent time.

Then many members of the game family came to call on Lucy. They, too, came ready for play. Yes, there is nothing in the world that a game is more ready for than a good play.

Then people came to see Lucy, too, and congratulate her on the fact that her sore throat had gone away for good.

A lovely gray felt bunny and a brown felt monkey always were with Lucy. They had always belonged to her and, though new visitors came, they did not leave her. The monkey put his arm around the bunny and with his other arm on the pillow by Lucy he looked most comfortable.

He hadn't left her all the time that she lay sick in her bed. He had been such a comfort. While she drank her soup, and when the doctor came to call, and when Mommy told her comforting stories to help her get well, the monkey was tucked as neat as you please under Lucy's arm.

"Well," he was saying to the gray rabbit, "I'm laughing up my sleeve."

"How can you do that?" asked the rabbit. "You haven't any sleeve and you aren't laughing up your arm. You're not even turning your mouth in that direction.

"What do you mean by saying that?"

"Oh, it is just an expression," said the monkey. "When

creatures say they're laughing up their sleeve it does not really mean that they're holding open their sleeve and saying:

"'Ha, ha, ha,' up it. But it means they're laughing inwardly or to themselves or so no one can see their laughter. That is what the expression means.

"So, you see no one can see my laughter, but I'm laughing all right because even though that mean old sore throat would have liked to stay, he couldn't, because Lucy wanted to get well.

Just then there came another visitor. This time it was the prince of desserts—Prince Ice-Cream. Proudly the Prince came in on the best and most royal of saucers. Hurray!

THE TIRED EAGLES

"IN THE house where Kenneth lived there was a chair which had always fascinated him. It was a very, very old chair, and Kenneth's mother and daddy were very proud of it," said daddy to Jack and Evelyn. "Kenneth's daddy had bought it at a sale of old and curious things. It was a Roman chair, and on either side were two heads of eagles. These four heads in all always made Kenneth wonder, for they looked so very life-like. He used to imagine that even little wooden eagles must get very tired of always being just the same. And late one afternoon, sitting in the chair he fell asleep.

"'You're terribly tired, aren't you?' said the first eagle, who suddenly seemed to be looking at him.

"'Yes, I'm a little tired,' Kenneth admitted.

"'Well, you're not as tired as we are,' said the second eagle.

"'No, indeed! said the third eagle. 'You're only tired because you've played so many games. We're tired because we're always still.'

"Kenneth listened eagerly, because he'd so often thought just what he was hearing. 'Yes,' said Kenneth very sympathetically, 'I should think you would be very dull. I've often thought that. Have you been there a long time?'

38

"'Oh, ages and ages!' replied the fourth eagle, who up to this time had not spoken. 'We were very old before your daddy got us. We've been on this chair so long. We can't remember how long. And what makes us feel so sad is that we are called eagles and should fly and yet are forever glued to this chair.'

"'Kenneth, Kenneth,' cried Kenneth's mother, 'it's long past bedtime!'

"'Oh, I am not so tired as the eagles are!' said Kenneth. And Kenneth's mother wondered if he was talking in his sleep."

The Story Garden

BETTY'S POSY SHOP

ONE early spring morning Betty found beside her plate many wee envelopes with flower pictures on them.

They rattled delightfully, and Betty tore open a corner of one and saw many tiny seeds.

"It's for your own little garden plot, dear," said Mother.

"My own little garden plot," echoed Betty. "Am I to have one?"

"You certainly are," and Betty found it to be true, for when she ran out, there it was. A bed of rich earth all raked over so fine and black just waiting.

She also found a cunning set of garden tools, and a pair of overalls, which she quickly put on, and behold! she was the dearest little gardener anyone ever saw.

Mother showed her how deep to plant the seeds, then covered them up in their little warm beds.

"I see a shower is coming," she said. "That will give them a drink before they go to sleep. When they waken you will see them pop up their little heads, and they will grow and grow just like little girls and boys."

Betty did not have to wait long to see their little heads peeping up, wearing tender little green bonnets, and she also saw something else peeping up that she never planted. These weeds weren't given time to grow but were pulled at once.

Every day she worked and by and by her little garden was a beautiful sight.

Father had placed a trellis for the baby rose, and the sweet peas seemed to fairly sing for joy as they climbed their ladder, filling the air with their perfume.

She also had old-fashioned flowers which seemed to say, "No matter what new-fangled flowers you have, we are always to be depended upon and make the sweetest corner in the garden."

Besides the flowers Betty found some of those seeds came up vegetables, and great fun she had each day making a surprise dish for dinner. These she covered with a napkin, and Father and Mother had to guess what was there.

Sometimes it was a few radishes, again a plate of crisp lettuce appeared. Once it was a dish of peas sweet as sugar.

One day Betty came running in much excited.

"Mother," she cried, "all the children are having shops, selling things. They are raising money to send poor little children to the country for a week. Can't I have a shop?"

"To be sure. What kind of shops are they having?"

"Some are selling lemonade; some ice-cream; some just peanuts. What do you think I could sell?"

"The very best thing any one ever did sell! You have so many flowers, why not make them into old-fashioned bouquets and sell to the passersby?" replied Mother.

This delighted the child's heart and each morning found her picking the dew-wet flowers and arranging them.

Father set up a small tent on the lawn, and there, looking like

BETTY'S POSY SHOP

a posy herself, she sat beside a small table filled with the nose-
gays which everyone loves.

A goodly sum she raised, and a jolly crowd of children had a
rollicking time just because of those envelopes found beside Betty's plate one lovely spring day.

> In little Betty's garden
>   Grew all sorts of posies.
> There were pinks and mignonettes
>   And tulips and roses.
>
> There the bee went for honey
>   And the humming birds, too,
> And there the pretty butterflies
>   And the ladybirds flew.
>
> Sweet peas and morning-glories,
>   Beds of violets blue,
> Marigolds, and asters,
>   In Betty's garden grew.
>
> And there among the flowers
>   One bright and pleasant day
> In her own pretty garden
>   Little Betty went to play.

HOW THE SNOWDROP CAME

SPRING seemed later than usual one year and there was a great stir among the little plants under the ground. They had been waiting patiently—so patiently—beneath the dark earth.

"I'm surely not mistaken," said one little plant to another beside it. "Spring has always been here earlier than this. I'm so anxious to grow. Indeed, I'd be satisfied to push just one small leaf above the ground."

"That would be nonsense, I assure you, for it's very cold still. The winter fairies just told me that some patches of snow can still be seen upon the hillsides."

"Why need we wait for the snow to go? I shouldn't mind if I did shiver a little. Anything is better than waiting under this dark ground."

It was a brave little plant that spoke and it meant just what it said; for, the next morning, one tiny blade of green had pierced its way through the hard ground. There it stood shivering alone in the great wide world.

"I'll not be so lonesome to-morrow," it said. "Many others will follow when they see how I have braved the cold." The next morning the ground was covered with slender green shoots.

It takes old Winter a long time to make up his mind to leave; and this time he was in no hurry to go, even when he saw that some tiny plants had bravely pushed their heads above the ground.

HOW THE SNOWDROP CAME

"This is quite a garden of green," said the winter fairies who, with anxious eyes, had been watching the little plants. "I do hope you will soon bloom, for it would be a great joy for us to see some blossoms before Winter takes us away."

"Alas! we have no blossoms," said one. "We could not have ventured out in the cold if we had had. Blossoms are very delicate, dear fairies. We can't hope for anything so beautiful."

There were some whisperings among the fairies, but the little plants could not make out what the little people were saying.

"Can we not plan some way to make them bloom?" whispered one fairy to another close beside her. "I should feel so happy to help."

"I have often thought a blossom made out of snow would be beautiful, so pure and white. But it would not last after Spring comes, I fear."

"The little plants may be glad of any blossoms. We can, at least, try."

In a few moments the fairies were at work. There were many plants to please, but the little fairies never stopped until they had shaped many balls of snow into beautiful white flowers such as the winter fairies loved best. These blossoms they hung on the slender green blades that had pushed themselves above the ground.

"What a garden of flowers!" called out one of the fairies. "If the plants can keep these blossoms until Spring comes we shall be repaid for our trouble." These blossoms, as you know, were not real, but the little plants never thought of that in their great happiness.

HOW THE SNOWDROP CAME

Spring came at last. The snow that had lain so long on the hillsides melted; and the snow-flowers, too, felt the warm breath.

"Well, my little plants," said Spring, "what brought you up so early? I wonder that you did not freeze!"

The plants lowered their heads.

"You do not seem pleased to see me. Are you not glad that I am here?" asked Spring.

"We are glad to see you—but our beautiful blossoms are gone. The winter fairies made them for us. We knew they must go as soon as you came and we could not help feeling sad when we knew you were here."

"The fairies made you blossoms of snow?" asked Spring in surprise. "Come, tell me all about it."

Then the little plants told how hard the winter fairies had worked to make each one of them a snow-flower and how dearly they had learned to love it.

"You shall still have blossoms," said Spring, "for you have been very brave to stay above the ground through this cold weather. I am late this year. It was time for you to be up."

"May our blossoms be like those the fairies made for us?" whispered one little plant.

In a few days the garden was abloom once more with blossoms pure and white—blossoms which did not melt.

"I shall call you my snowdrops," said Spring.

And the snowdrops have been brave ever since; for even to this day they may be seen pushing their heads above the winter ground—their dainty blossoms as white as the snow which often lies around them.

48

The Story Garden

Page 41

Betty's Posy Shop

Page 43

SNOWDROPS

Little ladies, white and green,
　　With your spears about you,
Will you tell us where you've been
　　Since we lived without you?

You are sweet, and fresh, and clean,
　　With your pearly faces;
In the dark earth where you've been,
　　There are wondrous places:

Yet you come again, serene,
　　When the leaves are hidden;
Bringing joy from where you've been,
　　You return unbidden.

Little ladies, white and green,
　　Are you glad to cheer us?
Hunger not for where you've been,
　　Stay till Spring be near us!

LAURENCE ALMA-TADEMA.

BETTY'S SURPRISE

IT WAS not often that Betty left the garden alone, but one bright day her little feet could be seen toddling down the road to a place where she remembered many flowers grew.

There was one little yellow dandelion that she loved best of all. She would have picked some of the bright-coloured blossoms of the little plant as she sat down beside it, if she had not heard a gentle voice say: "Betty, we're so glad to see you!"

"You dear little blossoms," she said, "I've watched you grow for a long time. Are you going to get any larger?"

"Oh, no, Betty, we're just going to enjoy the world now. We love the sunshine; we love the grass, and we love you, Betty, for we're sure you won't pick us."

"Would you feel very bad if some one should take you away?" asked the child.

"Very. We often tremble as old Mooly comes grazing near. One day she came so close that her warm breath made our leaves tremble. See, there she is now, coming toward us."

Mooly, as you may have guessed, was the old cow and she loved Betty dearly. As the gentle creature drew near she never thought of the dandelions, although they began trembling from head to foot.

"Don't mind, I'll send her away. Go back, Mooly, don't come here."

Mooly stood still and gazed at Betty with a kind, patient look, then turned and walked slowly back to the fields.

"I must go now."

"You will come again, Betty?"

But Betty was already a long way down the road, hurrying toward her home. It was several days before she visited the dandelions again.

As she walked slowly down the road several days later she heard a gentle voice say, "Here we are, Betty. I believe you have forgotten us."

"Dear me, I didn't know you, and no wonder! I was looking for beautiful yellow flowers and I find you gray-haired. Whatever has happened?"

"Well, Betty, we have just grown old—that's all."

"But it's only a few days since I saw you. There is not a bit of colour left! Would you have grown old so soon if I had picked you and kept you in a vase at home?"

"Perhaps not, but that would have been sad, indeed, for us, Betty. You know our family is very proud of its gray hair! We turn gray very young."

"I see," said Betty, quite surprised. "Won't you tell me what you are going to do now?"

"Of course, it's this way——"

"Whoo-oo-oo!" said Mr. Wind, and the dandelions' gray hairs were sprinkled all through the air.

"Oh! Oh!" cried Betty. "I wonder if he wished to have his hairs scattered in that way! Such funny things do happen."

And Betty ran back home.

51

THE FAIRY GARDENERS

"WHY are you watering that one little green spot, Betty?" asked her mother. "Why don't you water the flowers instead?"

Betty stopped watering, put down the pitcher, smiled until it looked as though her eyes were full of sunbeams, and answered, "It's a secret, promise you will never tell?"

"Never," answered her mother, smiling back at her.

"One day, quite a long time ago, as far back as last week," said Betty, "I heard a funny noise under the ground, just beneath the spot where I was watering. I put my ear down to the ground, like this." She knelt down and laid her ear upon the leaf still shining with drops from her pitcher.

"There, I hear the same sound again," she cried. "Only this time the words are different." She laughed and her mother heard a tiny answering laugh from under the ground.

"Listen!" cried Betty. "There is an elf or a brownie or a fairy down there! The first time I listened he was grumbling. I heard him say, 'All the roots of these plants are crying for water and there is not one drop left in the ground. What am I to do? Oh, dear, oh, dear!' And then he cried, he truly did, I heard him sobbing. Then suddenly he laughed and said, 'Well, my tears have watered the roots of that foxglove anyway! But, oh, dear, I can't cry any more—what shall I do?' Then I heard

52

him stamp with anger until the ground trembled under my ear.
So I ran and filled the milk pitcher, that I have for supper, with
water from the brook and watered just here where I heard the
elf. And every day since then I have watered in the same spot;
and then I listen and hear the elf singing to the plants as he
waters them. The words sound like this:

"'Here I come now, stop! stop! stop!'"

"Then I hear him watering.

"'Here I come now, hop! hop! hop!'"

"Then I hear him hopping on to the next place. Now isn't
that an exciting secret, Mother?"

Of course Mother thought it was, but the next day something
still more exciting happened.

Betty watered the green plant as usual, put her ear down to
the ground to listen, and heard the gay little voice singing nearer
and nearer:

"Here I come now, stop! stop! stop!
Here I come now, hop! hop! hop!"

Still nearer came the voice, right under the green leaf came
the sound of hopping. Then the words changed to,

"Here I come now, pop! pop!—pop!"

And right up through the ground, between the leaves, popped the merriest little elf you ever dreamed about. He was all dressed in brown, his eyes and skin and curly hair were brown, too, but as he shook the drops of water off his cap and bowed low to Betty she saw that slung over his back he carried a golden trowel and a diamond pitcher.

"Betty, my sweet little friend!" he cried, giving a funny little hop upon the leaf and turning a somersault upon it. "You see what no other child has ever seen, the Head Underground Gardener from this garden. Your old Scotch Gardener thinks he takes care of this garden, but really we—I and my assistants—do all the work! Still, if it hadn't been for you and your water pitcher, sweet Betty, we couldn't have kept these plants alive these last days! So now, as a reward, listen, look!"

The air was full of,

"Here we come now, hop! hop! hop!
Here we come now, stop! stop! stop!"

Betty looked around in wonder. Upon every green leaf stood a brown elf, each with his golden hoe and diamond watering pot.

"Hats on! Forward march!" commanded the Leader, the Head Underground Gardener, the one who had first spoken to Betty.

In a twinkling each elf had picked a foxglove blossom blue, white, yellow, and pink, put them on their heads, and were marching on the grass around Betty. The blossom hats were too big for them, they were put on very crookedly, and the mischievous little brown faces which looked out from under the gay hats **were** so funny and merry that Betty laughed with them.

"Present arms!" cried the Leader. Each elf took his golden hoe from his back and presented arms, the way soldiers do.

"Salute our flag!" commanded the Leader.

Betty gazed around wonderingly. Where was the flag? Then she looked back at the elves. Each one was saluting, with his tiny brown fingers, the golden sun which was setting gorgeously in the west.

"Shower of diamonds!" cried the Leader.

"Now what does he mean?" asked Betty to herself. But the elves knew. Each one held his diamond watering pot upside down, watering the green blades of grass in a circle around Betty with—a shower of diamonds! Betty knelt down and gathered handfuls of the glittering jewels and as she did so she heard, from the corner of the garden,

> "Here we go now, hop! hop! hop!
> Here——"

She looked around. The elves had disappeared and in her hands she held—nothing but drops of dew that dried in the sunbeams which fell upon her fingers.

"Oh, what a wonderful time I have had!" cried Betty. "I must run right off and tell Mother!"

Off she scampered—and this is the story she told!

LITTLE HOPTOAD'S FRIEND

LITTLE Hoptoad lived under a big rock in Tommy's garden. He often sat in his doorway and looked at the pretty lawn in front of his house.

"My garden is beautiful," he said one day. "Not a weed grows among the soft green grass."

One morning after breakfast he hopped out of his house to sit and blink in the sun. In the grass just in front of his home he saw something which shone like gold.

"I wonder what that is," he said. He hopped a few hops away from his door. Then he stopped and looked.

"A fluffy dandelion! And *right* in the middle of my garden. What does she mean? I'll go and ask her."

Just as he gave a big hop he heard the voices of children and the next moment Little Hoptoad was back in his home. Safe under the big rock he peeped out to watch three little children running about on the lawn blowing dandelion seeds in all directions.

"Oh, here's a fine one," cried one. Puffing out her cheeks she gave a long Whoo-oo-oo! And the children laughed as the gray hairs left the dandelion's head and flew this way and that over the lawn, and out to the fields beyond.

"Here's another," cried the second child. "I'll soon scatter his hairs. See if I don't. Whoo-oo-oo!" And the little gray hairs followed the others out of the garden, across the fields, anywhere and everywhere.

The third child spied the splendid dandelion which grew right in front of Little Hoptoad's home.

"Isn't this jolly?" he called out as his eye caught sight of the full round fluffy ball. She's the finest dandelion in the garden. Whoo-oo-oo," and he soon made short work of that downy head.

"Come," said one, "let's run into the field. I see some fine ones over there."

"We've blown the heads off of all these," was the answer; and away the children ran.

Little Hoptoad peeped out once more. Something in the garden looked very different.

"Humph!" he said, as soon as he noticed that fluffy dandelion was holding up a stalk with no downy ball on top. "They did make short work of that one. I wish they had blown her away, leaves and all, out of *my* garden. A few days ago she held up a yellow head; the next time I saw it it was gray; then it was white. But now all her hair is gone! It's plain to be seen that the children *don't* like her. Neither do I. What the saucy dandelion means by growing almost in front of my door is more than I can understand. I'll just hop over to her and tell her to get out of my garden as quickly as she can."

He soon reached the spot where the dandelion was growing.

"A nice-looking dandelion you are now with your hair all blown away. Why did you come to stay in *my* garden?"

"It is so nice and warm here," answered the dandelion. "I don't like shady places and the children *love* me."

"Humph!" said Little Hoptoad. "I wish you had not come. Besides, I don't call it loving you when they shake every hair off your head. That's what I saw a little boy do to you not a moment ago." And Little Hoptoad blinked and blinked as though he meant the dandelion to know that he was very angry.

But the dandelion laughed and laughed. "That's only fun," she said. "The children love to blow our hair away and we like it. Indeed, Little Hoptoad, if I may say so, it is *just* what we dandelions want."

"Well, if the children do like you, I *don't*. You spoil my garden. Every time I look out and take a peep—dear me, do I hear those children coming here again?" Little Hoptoad stopped and listened. He could hear the voices of the children as they ran from the field back into the garden. He was very much frightened. "I can't hop back to my home for they will see me. Dear me, dandelion, what shall I do?" Poor Little Hoptoad now looked up at dandelion as though she were the only friend he had.

"Hop under my leaves, and I'll cover you up," she said. "The children will never see you there. Be quick."

You may be sure Little Hoptoad lost no time in getting under dandelion's leaves; and, when the children reached the garden they did not dream that a little hoptoad was keeping very quiet under the broad green leaves of that splendid fellow whose head they had shaken just a few minutes before.

"What was it?" asked one child, looking all around.

"A little hoptoad—for I saw *him* and in *my* garden," said another.. "But where can he have gone?" asked the third child.

"Look around that rock. He may have hopped under there."

"If he did," said another, stooping down and looking, "we'll never catch him. Are you sure you saw a toad?"

"Of course I am—that is, I think I did—it certainly looked like one, a little one, right here in *my* garden."

"Well, he's gone now. Let's run back to the field, and blow some more dandelions. Come."

Away ran the children; but Little Hoptoad was too wise to put his head out from under dandelion's leaves until he was sure no one could see him.

"You're safe now, Little Hoptoad," called out dandelion. "The children have gone back into the field."

Little Hoptoad pushed out his head between the leaves, gave a big hop, then looked all around. "Thank you, dandelion," he said at last. "What beautiful leaves you have. They are so good to hide under. I don't believe I ever noticed them before. I shall come again to see you. Good day."

"Good day, Little Hoptoad," said dandelion, smiling.

THE WHITE BUTTERFLY

KITTY always said the butterfly awakened her. She was very tired that morning; her short, fat legs had trotted all over the house while she tried to help Mother. She was a little girl, but she was big enough to stand on the other side of the bed, smooth the clothes, and tuck them in. And when it came to dusting no one could reach the under parts of the chairs and tables so well as Kitty. Then when mother made a cake, it was great fun to get the egg beater and the big spoon and the pan. And when she said:

"Now, Kitty, you may shake in some more flour," the little girl felt that she was really making part of the cake. And when it was poured out in the pan she always had the big bowl in her lap to run her forefinger around and scrape up the sweet cake dough.

But that morning, after the cake was in the oven, she had trotted out under the apple tree and had lain down in the shadiest, softest spot in the grass. The next thing she knew a voice was saying:

"This is the most re-mark-a-ble thing I ever saw."

Kitty wondered deeply what it was. Then the voice said again:

"Most re-mark-a-ble."

Kitty opened her eyes and saw a white butterfly sitting on her arm.

"What is re-mark-a-ble?" she asked, and the white butterfly shot into the air as though he had been a balloon. In a moment or two he came fluttering back and flew round her head in circles.

"Re-mark-a-ble," he said again.

Kitty began to grow tired of the word. She sat up and said: "What is?"

The butterfly again made a balloon of himself; then he seemed to see there was nothing to fear from Kitty; so he alighted once more on her arm.

"You are," he said.

I am not," said Kitty. "I am just a little girl."

"A girl," said the butterfly, "a little girl. I never heard of such a thing."

"Well, I am," she answered. "Just a little girl and my name is Kitty Miller."

"Miller," repeated the butterfly. "Miller."

He looked at her very carefully and then he shook his head.

"No," he said. "I don't suppose you could be any kin to Moth Miller."

"Well, I'm not! Nasty little thing! He has so many crawly legs."

"Of course he has legs, six, as everybody ought to have. You, poor dear, have but two, I see. Unless," he added, "those other two things you wave around so are legs."

"They are not," said Kitty quite crossly, I am sorry to say. "They are my arms."

"Arms!" said the butterfly, "arms! I never heard of such a thing."

"Seems to me there is a great deal you never heard of," said Kitty. "When were you born?"

"Early this morning," answered the white butterfly, proudly. "Very early."

"This morning!" cried Kitty. "Why, then you are only a baby butterfly!"

"I am not!" said the butterfly, and his wings trembled, he spoke so firmly, "I am a full-grown butterfly, as anyone can see. But perhaps we would better talk about something else. Where are your wings?"

"My wings!" Kitty had never been so surprised. "Why, I haven't any wings."

"Oh, yes, you have," answered the butterfly. "You must have, you know. Feel around on your back and you'll find them."

Almost without thinking, Kitty's fat little hand went over her shoulders. Then she drew it back and said:

"I know there aren't any there. Little girls don't have wings."

"Little girls don't have wings!" repeated the butterfly. "Why, I never heard of such a thing."

"My mother says," went on the little girl, "that if I am very good I will have wings, some day."

"To be sure," said the butterfly, brightening, "when you come out of your cocoon. Now when," he asked politely, "do you go in?"

"I don't go into a cocoon at all," said Kitty.

"You don't! Well, I never heard—but perhaps we would better talk about something else," said the butterfly. "What do you think of the sky?"

"Oh, I love it," cried Kitty, taking peeps at it through the branches of the apple tree.

"It is so blue and bright."

"To be sure," said the butterfly, highly delighted, turning his head so he could take peeps at it, too.

"That's very good. Blue, and bright! So it is. I knew we should find something we both liked. Now what do you think of the clouds?"

"I think they are dear," answered Kitty, "soft and woolly, like little sheep in the meadow."

The butterfly could scarcely sit still, he was so excited.

"So they are!" he cried. "So they are! Like little sheep in the green meadows." Then he grew very grave and said:

"But did you think of that, now? The sky is blue and the meadows are green. Now sheep would not be in a blue meadow, you know."

"Of course not," said Kitty.

"Then why did you say so? But there, perhaps we would better talk about something else. What do you think of the flowers?"

"Oh, I love them best of all," answered Kitty, clapping her hands.

"So do I," said the butterfly. "How well we are getting on together. Now, which do you like best?"

"I believe I like the violets. They come so early."

"Yes," said the butterfly, "but a violet is rather small for two to sit on."

"Sit on?" cried Kitty. "Who wants to sit on a violet?"

The butterfly did not answer. "By the way, though," he said softly, "do you ever get lonely?"

"Oh, yes," sighed Kitty, "and I wish I had someone to play with."

"That's it," said the butterfly. "Some one to play with."

"Well, there are plenty of butterflies around here," Kitty said, looking into the garden.

"Yellow ones," answered the white butterfly. "I do not care to play with yellow butterflies."

"I think they are very pretty," the little girl said, "but if you don't like them there is a big white one on that big rose."

The butterfly almost fell off Kitty's arm. Then he spread his wings very wide and said:

"See here, you are my friend, aren't you?"

"Yes," she answered. "I don't know you very well, but I guess I am."

"How do I look? Are my feathers all smooth?"

"Your feathers? I didn't know you had feathers."

"Well, I have. Do I look all right?"

"You look lovely to me," said the little girl, and then the white butterfly flew into the air and Kitty heard him say:

"A rose! So nice and roomy for two."

And just then Mother called that the cake was done. "Come and see how lovely and brown it looks." Kitty did not want to go, and she hurried back again to the apple tree without even asking Mother for a slice. There, on the big red rose, sat two little white butterflies, but although she spoke to them more than once, neither answered. When she went too close they flew away over the meadows.

Kitty went back to the house with tears in her eyes and told Mother all about it. Mother only smiled and said she had been dreaming. Then she gave her a large piece of cake to comfort her. But Kitty never believed she was dreaming. What do you think?

THE LITTLE PLANT

On the edge of the forest stood a tiny plant. It was only six inches tall.

The ground around it was so cold and hard that it could not grow taller. It had stood there many years, sad and sorrowful.

"Grow and be beautiful," said the forest sternly; but the little plant did not grow.

"Do you not wish to grow?" asked a bluejay. Then he began to tell the little plant how lazy and useless it was. But his words went into one ear and out of the other.

Still the plant did not grow.

"Grow! Grow!" roared the wind. "Grow tall and straight. I will teach you to obey. Grow! Grow!"

Then the wind lashed the tiny plant, and beat its branches to the ground. But the poor thing came near dying and did not grow at all.

"Do grow," said the sun. "Grow and be beautiful. I will help you."

Then the sun warmed the earth around the plant, and gentle showers fell on it from the clouds.

Then the little twigs began to grow, and in time the tiny plant became a beautiful tree, with green leaves and snow-white bark.

PIXIE FLOWERS

ONCE upon a time there lived near a pixie-field a good old woman called Mother Bailey who had a cottage and a very pretty garden, where she cultivated the most beautiful bed of tulips. The pixies, it is said, so delighted in this spot that they would carry their elfin babies there and sing them to rest. Often at midnight a soft lullaby was heard and strains of the sweetest music would float in the air. It seemed to come from the beautiful tulips themselves. And while these delicate flowers waved their heads to the evening breezes it sometimes seemed as if they were marking time to their own singing. As soon as the elfin babies were lulled asleep by the sweet music, the pixies would return to their neighboring field, and there commence dancing, making those rings on the green, which showed even to mortal eyes, what kind of frolics the pixies had had during the midnight season.

At the first dawn of light the watchful pixies once more sought the tulips, and, although they could not be seen, they could be heard kissing and caressing their babies. The tulips so favoured by the pixies' visits remained beautiful much longer than any other flowers in the garden; and when the pixies breathed over them they became as fragrant as roses.

So delighted at all this was the good old woman who owned the garden that she never allowed a single tulip to be plucked from its stem. But when she died her cottage and garden be-

67

came the property of some one who did not love flowers as she did; and, in time, the new owner destroyed the beautiful bed and planted parsley in place of the enchanted tulips.

This so disappointed and offended the pixies that they caused the parsley to wither away. For many years, indeed, nothing would grow in any bed in the garden.

But every night before the moon was at the full they paid tribute to the old woman's memory by singing sweet songs around her grave. Then would they sing and dance and rejoice as they hailed the queen of the night complete her silver circle in the skies. No rank weeds were ever seen to grow upon the grave of good Mother Bailey who had guarded the tulip beds for the delight of those elfin creatures.

LITTLE EDITH'S GARDEN

"'WHATEVER shall I do?' said little Edith to herself," commenced daddy, "'I do want to have a garden so much and yet the snails eat it up!'

"While she was wondering like this a little voice whispered in her ear:

"'Edith, Edith,' it said.

"'Yes,' answered Edith looking about her. And then, seeing no one, said:

"'Who are you? Where are you?'

"'I'm the Fairy Queen,' said the voice, 'and you can't see me because I've put on my invisible robe—which no one can see but a Fairy. I've come to talk to you. I know how you love your garden and that you've not been able to make anything grow this summer. Listen!' And a queer swishing sound passed through the air.

"'There!' continued the Fairy Queen, 'I have waved my invisible wand and it will bring you luck. Do not plant any seeds for a week—then the snails will think you have decided not to have any garden at all! It will be a joke on them—but they have had enough feasts and now it is time for you to have a garden!'

LITTLE EDITH'S GARDEN

"In a short time Edith had real flowers, and her garden was more beautiful than ever it had been, and often when she was working among the flowers, she said half aloud:

"'If the Fairy Queen is around me in her invisible robe, I want to thank her, oh, so much, for my lovely garden.'"

SAVING THE ELM

"YES, I was very, very ill," said the elm tree. "I didn't know whether I would ever get well or not. I had all sorts of things the matter with me. My wood was cracking and I was generally in bad shape.

"They talked about me, people did, and they said it would be a great pity to cut me down. They said I gave shade in the hot summer, they said I was very beautiful and they said I should be saved if possible. A lot of very clever tree doctors were sent for and they said that I could be saved. Oh, how happy that made me!" And Grandfather Elm swayed in the breeze and smiled.

"All the bad wood which had started in to hurt me was taken away. Then they fixed up the places where the old wood had been so it would keep in good condition in the future.

"I had steel straps put upon me in certain places to keep me from blowing over and fixed in such a way that I could sway and laugh and blow naturally with the rest of you.

"My, but when they said I was all right, how I did rejoice! I was so happy, so happy. For I am a well elm now!"

71

THE GARDEN TOOLS

"IT'S GREAT fun to be a rake," said the rake, "and to make everything look nice and tidy. And in the autumn it is such fun raking up all the leaves and getting ready for the big bonfires.

"It is fun, too, to rake the freshly mown grass and to make everything smooth and nice."

"Ah, but it is such fun to be a trowel," said the trowel, "and to dig around the garden flowers and to make them grow. They like to be made all nice and comfy, to have the dirt loosened about them to give them a little breathing space.

"They don't like too much! They want to be held in the earth firmly but with soft, nicely pressed earth about them. And our family attends to that."

"Ah, but it is nice to be a hoe," said the hoe, "for I can do such a great deal of work. Just take the work I do with string-beans alone.

"I don't suppose there could be any string-beans if it weren't for me. I do such a great deal with the string-beans. I keep them cheerful. I pay them some attention. I make them feel like growing up into nice vegetables. I hoe all about them."

72

THE GARDEN TOOLS

"But think of all the help I am when any one wants to transplant anything," said the trowel. "I can dig up the root so that plenty of its dirt comes up with it. Plants don't like to leave all their soil behind; they like to take a little of it along with them, just as people do when they're going away for the summer—they like to take along with them some of their photographs and little odds and ends, some of the things near and dear to them."

"It is the same way with the plants and I help to make that possible."

"Well," said the lawn-mower, "I like to make the lawn and the terraces look nice and I do make them look so neat. I'm the lawn's barber, I am!"

All the other garden tools moved about and laughed in their funny tool way at the joke the lawn-mower had tried to crack.

"Pretty good, pretty good," they said.

"And a garden fork like me," said the garden fork, "can do a good deal of work too. I like to do my share."

"We can do a good deal," said several balls of string. "We keep things from falling down and we give them a little help and encouragement."

"So do we," said some little sticks up which some plants were climbing.

"We try to do our part," said a little two-pronged fork and a shovel together.

A two-pronged fork is a fork with two prongs instead of three or four as a fork usually has, you will notice.

"But I feel as if I were a great deal of help these days,"

said the hoe, "just when those string-beans need so much attention."

"And I must thin out some of the flowers," said the trowel. "Some of them are growing so closely together that they won't live that way and so I am going to separate them and put them in other beds."

"And you will need my help, too," said the watering pot, "not to mention the water!"

"That is so," said the trowel. "But I have a great deal of important weeding to do."

"And I will have to rake up the weeds that you have dug up in the garden path," said the rake, "or things won't look tidy and neat."

"And I must water all the flowers for there hasn't been any rain in some time and it's up to me to do a great deal of work," said the watering pot.

"I really think," said the rake, "that we are all useful. We all help the one who owns the garden. Yes, every one of us helps.

"We must all work, each do his part, for each one is needed for something or other."

"You're right," said the hoe; "none of us should boast alone. We should all work together for the good of the garden and for the good of the flowers. Then we will each be doing more, for when creatures and things work together and don't waste time boasting and arguing then a lot gets finished."

Cheerful Stories

THE SEA BLOSSOM

ONCE, not so very long ago, there grew upon the sands at the bottom of the sea a strange golden flower. It was like a great tulip bud tightly closed, but so full of golden light that it shone through the green water until the fishes saw it for miles away and swam to it, wriggling their noses with excitement and flapping their tails.

"What is it? What can it be?" they asked. "For flowers like ours do not grow under the sea, and the sea-anemones we read about are really quite horrid plants which catch and eat up little fishes." Soon all the sea folk were talking about this strange and beautiful flower. Crabs, lobsters, jelly-fish, big and little fishes chattered and questioned. But most of all it was loved by the mermaids. There were always several of them swimming around it, touching it carefully with their dainty fingers and sniffing at it with their pretty turned-up noses, for it was as fragrant as a whole flower garden—and in the sea nothing smells of anything except a nice clean saltiness.

"Bring the golden flower to my palace and plant it in my throne room!" commanded the Sea King.

So about a hundred little mermaids dug down in the sand with big shells for spades, while all the fish stood upon their tails with excitement, nodding their heads and begging to help. When at last the mermaids dug out the long white roots and lifted up the wonderful plant, the crabs clapped their claws with delight and the fish waved back and forth upon their tails until they fell over backward in a shining heap, giggling with pleasure.

But a still more thrilling moment soon came. When the blossom stood, firmly planted by the mermaids, in the sand of the splendid throne room, when the King, Queen, sea-folk, and mermaids were flapping with their tails—which they do instead of clapping as we do the hands—what do you suppose happened?

The golden bud opened! Slowly its petals folded back and there, lying in the very heart, lay—a tiny baby boy!

Such a flapping of tails had never been heard in the sea before. They made such a noise that the boys and girls playing above on the beach stood still and asked, "Is that thunder?" But beneath the sea, in the palace of the Sea King, the noise was terrific.

"What is it?" "It has no tail!" "It has queer sticks where its tail ought to be!" the sea-folk cried, crowding around until the King ordered them all back for fear the baby would be smothered. Indeed, the child had begun to give a funny little whimpering cry, a sound never before heard below the sea. A sweet little mermaid with a green tail and streaming locks swam forward and picked the baby up in her white arms. He stopped crying at once, smiled and laughed and—began to grow! He grew until he was the size you see him in the picture, his smocks as golden as the blossom, and the mermaid had to put him down and take his chubby hand.

"Look! He stands on those funny sticks!" cried the fish,

while the boy stepped forward and held out his hand politely to the Sea King.

"Please," said the little lad, "I think I'll go home now." "Home? What is that?" echoed the mermaids and the fish. The boy looked as though he were going to cry again, then he smiled and his smile seemed to fill the sea with sunbeams.

"Why, home is on the land you see," he said. "I was wading, and the waves tried to catch my feet and I said, 'If you catch them you will have to take me to the bottom of the sea and show me the mermaids that my mother tells me about.' And they did catch me and they carried me away and I must have gone to sleep—and now, you are all very nice but if you don't mind I guess little boys are meant to live on land and I'm very hungry!"

"Feed him! Feed him!" cried the mermaids, swimming over to the Sea King's coral side-table. Dishes, or shells, filled with food for the King's supper were spread out upon it. The mermaids lifted them and swam quickly to the lad.

"See, here is whipped Sea Foam!" they cried. "And here are Sand Cookies and Sea Weed Custard!"

The boy tasted them and shook his head. "I want bread and butter and jam," he said. "And I want to go home, I don't like the way the lobsters look at me!"

Indeed, the lobsters were stretching out their claws very crossly and the crabs looked so angry that their eyes were fairly popping out of their shells.

"You people like to eat *us!*" they cried. "We know what you are—you are nothing but a human being!"

"Yes, yes!" cried the fishes. "You are the worst kind of

human being, you are a boy! Boys catch us with hooks! We will show him what it feels like to be caught!"

They all swam at him angrily, and if the little mermaid had not caught him up in her arms and swam very fast up to the beach and thrown him onto the sand—why, if she *had not,* you would never have heard this story!

But she did and the fishes and lobsters and crabs got there too late, and so the boy is still playing on the beach every warm day, letting the waves come almost to his toes, but never quite, never near enough to catch them and carry him back to the palace of the Sea King!

The Fairy Gardeners

Page 52

Cheerful Stories

Page 75

NICK BLUSTER'S TRICK

ONE bright day Nick Bluster was rollicking about Sweet Brier Dell in the merriest kind of way. Every now and then he stopped to hold his sides, for he was shaking with laughter. In fact, he was laughing so hard that he could not answer his friend Jack Frost, who shouted out at the top of his voice, "Where are you going, Nick Bluster?"

Nick could do nothing but nod his head and laugh. This made Jack very suspicious, so he stopped and said, "Now, Nick Bluster, you're going to play some trick. What is it? Come, tell me."

"It's a secret, Jack. Ha! Ha! Ha!"

"But you'll tell me?" said Jack Frost, coming close.

Merry Nick put one finger on his lips and looked all around the hollow. "Hush!" he whispered. "Are you sure Old King Winter is gone? He must not see us with our heads together. He'll suspect mischief, Jack."

"Ho, nonsense! Of course he's gone. Come, Nick, you aren't going to keep a good bit of fun from me, are you? I'm always ready to share with you," pouted Jack Frost.

Nick Bluster put his head very near Jack's ear and whispered something.

"You needn't be afraid to talk here in the hollow," said Jack, impatiently.

"All right," laughed Nick. "I know how to have some jolly good fun! Old King Winter has sent his annual message to the Queen of Spring. He told her that he needed a long rest, therefore, he would go north a little earlier than usual this year. Ha! Ha! Ha! Oh, Jack! Ha! Ha! Ha!"

"Do stop your laughing and tell me how you are to have fun, Nick," said Jack. "I know about King Winter's message. What has that to do with your fun? I heard Bleak Blizzard, Snowdrift, Sleet, and Hail all say they were glad enough to leave. No doubt they've done good service for three months. Come, are you going to tell me? If not, I shall have some fun by myself."

"I'll tell you, Jack, and you shall help me. The Queen of Spring was very glad, of course, to receive King Winter's message. She and her handmaidens are planning a wildflower pageant. It is to be on the first of May, I think. They are to meet together at noon in Sweet Brier Hollow, where they will make millions of spring blossoms. What say you, Jack, to a jolly good trick on my Lady Spring and her handmaidens?"

"There's nothing I'd like better," said Jack Frost, who was now thoroughly interested. "Tell me your plan, Nick."

"Oh, Jack, it will be easy. You and I will hide in that thicket of saplings. When the Queen and her maidens are busily at work making the blossoms, we will rush out and——"

Jack Frost could not wait. He burst into the merriest laugh and cried out, "I see, I see! Ha! ha! ha!"

But Nick wanted to finish his story, so he went on: "Jack, my friend, you'll skip about with your icicle wand and touch each maiden's nose. Can't you hear them cry out? 'Oh, oh! Ouch, ouch!' What fun it will be, Jack."

"And you'll rush about and blow your icy breath into their faces. So!" and Jack puffed his cheeks and blew as hard as he could.

Nick nodded his head. "I'll do more than that. I'll scatter their flowers to the ends of Sweet Brier Dell. Listen! I believe I hear singing. Come, come, Jack! Slip into the thicket and wait."

The noisy little friends had barely time enough to run behind the bushes when into full view danced Merry Sunshine all clad in softest gold. She was leading the Queen of Spring and several of her Majesty's handmaidens. The fair queen wore a robe of delicate green, and on her head was a many-coloured coronet of dewy blossoms. Morning Mist in palest rose colour, Silver Shower in soft, warm gray, Evening Dew in rainbow tints followed, and each handmaiden carried a basketful of flower petals. As they danced after Merry Sunshine they sang:

"Come dance with me in Sweet Brier Dell,
    Fair maidens blithe and gay,
The graceful Queen of joyous Spring
    Begins her reign to-day.

"To gladden little children dear,
    A wildflower pageant bright
Shall deck the fields and banks and bowers,
    To give young hearts delight."

In a short time the Queen of Spring and her helpers reached the spot where they were to make blossoms. The Queen took her place on a mossy throne, and the handmaidens placed the baskets of petals at her feet.

"This year the dear children shall have plenty of flowers,— enough, I assure you, to satisfy them," said the Queen.

"I'm glad Old King Winter left early," laughed Merry Sunshine.

"Skip over to South Breeze's cave, Merry Sunshine, and tell her we are here a little earlier than usual. Also, say that she need have no fear of blustering North Wind," said the Queen.

Then her Majesty turned to Silver Shower and said, "Call the little brook, my dear. I long to hear its gurgle once more."

In a very short time Merry Sunshine brought gentle South Breeze, clad in the palest blue robe, to join the others.

They were all ready now to begin the work of making blos·· soms.

"What was that?" asked the Queen, looking sharply at a neighbouring thicket. "I thought I heard a sharp rustle."

"Surely that rude blusterer, North Wind, is not here. I dare not blow my warm breath until he is gone," said South Breeze.

"The very thought of him makes me shiver," sighed Silver Shower.

"He's not half as bad as that mischievous Jack Frost," whispered Evening Dew. "I'm very much afraid of him."

"And so am I," declared Morning Mist. "Last year I remember——"

Another rustle in the thicket attracted all the handmaidens' attention again.

"Come, let us begin," said the Queen. "Here are plenty of petals. Choose whatever you like, for each of you may make your favourite blossoms."

"Daffodils for me, dear Queen," said Merry Sunshine. "Daffodils with trumpets of pure gold. And I'll make dandelions, too, and buttercups—the children's own flower, for the meadows."

"My choice is crocus flowers—of many colours—white and gold, violet and rich purple," said Morning Mist, selecting her petals from the baskets.

"I shall make pink and white Mayflowers, to cover the hedges," said Silver Mist. "Evening Dew, what is your choice?"

"Violets for every nook in the dell. What a delight they are to the children!" said Evening Dew.

South Breeze chose to make hyacinth bells for shady groves. All were soon busy at work, singing and making exquisite blossoms.

There was a crackling of branches; a gust of wind; a burst of rollicking laughter. Nick Bluster, with his cheeks puffed out, and Jack Frost, carrying an icicle wand, rushed from the thicket. The Queen and her handmaidens shivered. "Oh! Oh! Oh!" they cried as Jack Frost touched each dainty nose with his icicle wand! Puff! Puff! Puff! blew Nick Bluster, and away to the ends of the dell scattered the lovely petals and blossoms.

In a moment the Queen saw who the intruders were. "What does this mean?" she demanded.

"Jack Frost! North Wind! Nick Bluster! Oh! Oh! Oh!"

cried the handmaidens. The mischief was done, and away ran the rollicking chaps back to their hiding place.

How indignant the Queen was! "Come!" she commanded. "Let's away. Old King Winter has not taken all of his attendants. He has left the two sauciest ones. But I'll not put up with such rudeness. Come! There shall be no spring this year! Away! Away!"

"I beg your Majesty to come to my cave. The rude fellows can do us no harm there," said gentle South Breeze.

"To the cave of South Breeze!" ordered the Queen. "There shall be no spring this year."

Away went the Queen and her attendants. But as soon as they had gone, out from the thicket stepped Jack and Nick.

"Did you hear what the Queen said, Nick Bluster? There'll be no spring this year!" said Jack Frost, nodding his head.

"She didn't mean it, Jack," said Nick, in a frightened voice.

"Oh, yes, she did! No spring this year! The brook is already beginning to gurgle over the pebbles and I hear the birds are on their way. You know Old King Winter sent his message to the Queen of Spring," said Jack Frost.

"What shall we do?" asked Nick.

"It's all your fault, Nick," said Jack Frost. "It was your idea to play this trick."

Nick looked frightened. "Let's slip away to the Northland, Jack," he said.

"What an idea! Old King Winter will suspect us of playing tricks if there's no spring, Nick. It's your fault."

"But, Jack, I did it just for fun. We must beg the Queen

86

to come out of that cave. Help me to think of a plan, Jack, do."

"They say she's very stubborn if once she's offended, Nick. See here! You'll have to mend your ways, you're entirely too mischievous."

"Jack Frost, you like a bit of fun as much as I do. Please help me out of this trouble. You're a clever fellow, Jack. Can't you think of a plan?" pleaded Nick.

Jack thought for a moment or two. Then he said, "They say the Queen of Spring is very proud of her grace and beauty. Listen, Nick. From the bank of the brook which flows near the cave of South Breeze I'll pretend to greet a water nymph who dwells in the depths of the stream. I'll praise her beauty and grace. I'll tell her she's more beautiful than the Queen of Spring. And I'll beg her to come and be Queen of Spring."

Nick didn't quite follow Jack's plan: so he asked, "Suppose she won't come?"

"Of course she won't come, stupid. She won't even show her face to me. But don't you see that my words will make the offended Queen jealous and she'll want to see the nymph? When her Majesty comes out of the cave——" Jack's eyes twinkled merrily and Nick Bluster saw through the plan.

"Oh! I see! Ha! ha! ha!" he cried.

Jack Frost slipped away to carry out his plan. He ran to the brook, leaned over to look deep into it, and called out, "Nick Bluster, Nick Bluster! Do come here and see the most beautiful sight in the whole world."

In a moment Nick was kneeling beside his little friend. "What is it you see, Jack?"

"Look!" said Jack, pointing down. "In the brook is a water nymph, the loveliest creature I've ever seen. See, she wears a coronet of wild flowers in her bright hair and her robe is made of lacy ferns. She is beautiful enough to be the Queen of Spring."

"How gracious she looks!" said Nick. "What a lovely coronet of flowers!"

"She is the Queen of Spring, Nick," cried Jack. "Perhaps we were deceived. Come, I'm ready to join Old King Winter, now."

"So am I. Let's hasten away," said Nick. But they hid in the thicket again.

Now, of course, the Queen and her handmaidens heard the conversation about the nymph who was beautiful enough to be the Queen of Spring, and as soon as the two merry chaps were out of sight, the Queen said to her maidens, "What did those two clowns say? I can't believe my own ears."

"Let us go over to the brook and see if the nymph is as beautiful as your Majesty," said Merry Sunshine. "I don't believe it."

"We'll all go quickly and look. Then we'll hasten back into the cave."

The Queen and her maidens hastened to the edge of the brook. Her Majesty leaned over and looked into the depths of the clear water.

"What does your Majesty see?" asked the anxious handmaidens.

"Alas! 'Tis true! Here dwells a lovely nymph. Look!"

The handmaidens peered into the brook to see the nymph,

when, lo! they discovered that her Majesty was looking at her own likeness mirrored by the clear water.

" 'Tis your Majesty's own image which we see. Jack Frost and Nick Bluster have tricked us again," said Morning Mist.

"And look! There they stand in the door of South Breeze's cave. We cannot go back. What shall we do?" asked Merry Sunshine.

In a moment Nick Bluster stepped forward and said, "O Queen of Spring, we humbly beg your pardon. It is indeed your own sweet image which you see in the brook."

"Forgive us, gracious Queen," added Jack Frost, bowing. "Let me explain. It was all a little joke. We were having a bit of fun. Never again will we meddle with your plans. If you will stay and make your blossoms, we'll hurry off to the north."

Jack was becoming frightened, for the Queen looked stern and unforgiving. Presently he added, "For the children's sake will you forgive us?"

"What say my handmaidens?" asked the Queen.

With one voice they answered, "For the children's sake, let us forgive them."

Off ran Nick and Jack as fast as they could. When they were near the edge of Sweet Brier Dell they heard merry voices singing:

"To gladden little children dear,
 A wildflower pageant bright
Shall deck the fields and banks and bowers,
 To give young hearts delight."

MAGNIFICAT AND TIBBY

"So THAT's where he lives," said Tibby. "It's in a tiny house out on the lawn. How fine!"

She pricked up her ears, then lowered her head to take a peep under the gate at a handsome Angora cat quietly lapping milk from a large bowl set out on the lawn before him. "And I am sure that he has all the milk he wants to drink."

Tibby, as you may have guessed, was a little kitten. Every day since she had once seen Magnificat sitting on the fence post basking in the sun, she had thought and thought about him. She wondered where he lived, and how he caught his mice, and just how much milk he had to drink.

"I'll find out for myself," she said one day. "He doesn't live far from here." So Tibby ventured out of her yard and across the road as far as the gate. And there was Magnificat in all his glory!

"A bowl *full* of milk," she said as she watched him drink as much as he wanted, lick his chops slowly, then lie down and begin to doze.

"I'm not afraid," said Tibby. She slipped under the gate across the lawn and almost to where the cat lay. For some time she stood looking at him.

"He is beautiful," she said to herself. "He does live in a fine way. And he has all the milk he wants to drink." Tibby then took a peep into the bowl. *"And more!"* she called out when she found the bowl still half-full.

"What's that?" asked Magnificat sleepily, as he slowly opened his large yellow eyes.

Tibby did not mean that he should hear what she was saying.

"Oh, Sir," said Tibby, half afraid, "I did not mean to waken you, indeed, I did not, Sir."

"What is that you say?" asked the cat again, when he caught sight of the little kitten before him.

"I was just saying that you live in a fine way and have all the milk you want to drink—and more."

"Oh," said Magnificat, yawning. "Oh, yes, they bring me plenty of milk so long as I'm tied here. Don't you get any?"

"Sometimes," said Tibby. "I belong to a poor little girl across the road, so I get milk only once in a while. Often I have to hunt a mouse for my dinner."

"Hunt a mouse? I call that fun," said Magnificat.

"But I'd rather live as you do and have all the milk I want to drink."

"Nonsense," said Magnificat, "you don't know what you are talking about. Do you know how it feels to be tied to one place by a chain?"

"No," said Tibby.

"Do you know what it means never to have even a chance at a mouse?"

"No," said Tibby.

"I thought you didn't. That's why I say you don't know what you are talking about."

"Perhaps not," said Tibby, "but I must go now and catch a mouse."

"I should like to have a chance," said Magnificat, as he watched Tibby scamper away across the lawn and slip under the garden gate.

Tibby didn't go back to see Magnificat for several days and when she did, she found the door of his little house open and Magnificat gone. She ran round and round, peeping here and there, and feeling for all the world as if she were as handsome as Magnificat and living in just such a fine way.

"I'll go inside his house and drink some milk," said Tibby. As she went in her tail brushed against the door. Snap! The door closed with a spring!

"It is fine to live as he did. Now I shall have all the milk I want to drink—and more." Tibby looked into the large bowl left in the corner, but it was empty.

"Oh, they'll bring some milk to me just as they did to him." And she jumped up and down and purred as if she thought herself the finest kitten in the world.

But no one came to the little house, for no one had seen Tibby go in; and soon the little kitten grew tired, then hungry. She made up her mind at last that she would wait no longer for the milk, but would go back to her own home.

But when she tried to get out she found the door locked. She called out a hungry, faint little "mew, mew." But no one came. Tired Tibby then fell asleep and slept all night long.

Daylight came and wakened the hungry kitten. "If some one would only come and take me out," was her first thought. "I'll call again; I'll call out as loud as I can this time." She was hungry and frightened, too, but she called out "mew, mew," with all the voice she had. And then came an answer, "Tibby, Tibby, where are you?"

Another faint "mew, mew," brought a little girl running to the tiny house. "Oh, Tibby, have you been there all the time? How did you get in there, my Tibby?"

The little girl opened the door and out jumped Tibby, who, you may be sure, scampered off home as fast as she could go. And Tibby never said a word to anyone about Magnificat.

THE TRAVELING MUSICIANS

An HONEST farmer had once a donkey, that had been a faithful servant to him a great many years, but was now growing old and every day more and more unfit for work. His master, therefore, was tired of keeping him and began to think of putting an end to him; but the donkey, who saw that some mischief was in the wind, took himself slyly off, and began his journey towards the great city. "There," thought he, "I may turn musician."

After he had traveled a little way, he spied a dog lying by the roadside and panting as if he were very tired.

"What makes you pant so, my friend?" asked the donkey.

"Alas!" said the dog, "my master was going to knock me on the head, because I am old and weak, and can no longer make myself useful to him in hunting; so I ran away; but what can I do to earn my livelihood?"

"Hark ye!" said the donkey, "I am going to the great city to turn musician: suppose you go with me, and try what you can do in the same way?"

The dog said he was willing, and they jogged on together.

They had not gone far before they saw a cat sitting in the middle of the road and making a most rueful face.

"Pray, my good lady," said the donkey, "what's the matter with you—you look quite out of spirits?"

"Ah me!" said the cat. "How can one be in good spirits when one's life is in danger? Because I am beginning to grow old, and had rather lie at my ease by the fire than run about the house after the mice, my mistress laid hold of me, and was going to drown me; and though I have been lucky enough to get away from her, I do not know what I am to live upon."

"Oh!" said the donkey. "By all means go with us to the great city; you are a good night-singer, and may make your fortune as a musician."

The cat was pleased with the thought, and joined the party.

Soon afterwards—as they were passing by a farmyard—they saw a cock perched upon a gate, and screaming out with all his might and main.

"Bravo!" said the donkey. "Upon my word you make a famous noise; pray what is this about?"

"Why," said the cock, "I was just now saying that we should have fine weather for our washing-day, and yet my mistress and the cook don't thank me for my pains, and threaten to cut off my head to-morrow, and make broth of me for the guests that are coming on Sunday!"

"Heaven forbid!" said the donkey. "Come with us, Master Chanticleer; it will be better, at any rate, than staying here to have your head cut off! Besides, who knows? If we take care to sing in tune, we may get up some kind of concert, so come along with us."

"With all my heart," said the cock; so they all four went on jollily together.

They could not, however, reach the great city the first day;

so when night came on, they went into a wood to sleep. The donkey and the dog laid themselves down under a great tree, and the cat climbed up into the branches; while the cock, thinking that the higher he sat the safer he should be, flew up to the very top of the tree, and then, according to his custom, before he went to sleep, looked out on all sides of him to see that everything was well. In doing this, he saw afar off something bright and shining, and, calling to his companions, said: "There must be a house no great way off, for I see a light."

"If that be the case," said the donkey, "we had better change our quarters, for our lodging is not the best in the world!"

"Besides," added the dog, "I should not be the worse for a bone or two, or a bit of meat."

So they walked off together towards the spot where Chanticleer had seen the light; and as they drew near, it became larger and brighter, till they at last came close to a house in which several robbers lived.

The donkey, being the tallest of the company, marched up to the window and peeped in.

"Well, Donkey," said Chanticleer, "what do you see?"

"What do I see," replied the donkey; "why, I see a table spread with all kinds of good things, and robbers sitting round it making merry."

"That would be a noble lodging for us," said the cock.

"Yes," said the donkey, "if we could only get in."

So they consulted together how they should contrive to get the robbers out; and at last they hit upon a plan. The donkey placed himself upright on his hind-legs, with his fore-feet resting against the window; the dog upon his back; the cat scrambled up to the dog's shoulders, and the cock flew up and sat upon the cat's head. When all was ready, a signal was given, and they began their music. The donkey brayed, the dog barked, the cat mewed, and the cock screamed; and then they all broke through the window at once, and came tumbling into the room, amongst the broken glass, with a hideous clatter! The robbers, who had been not a little frightened by the opening concert, had now no doubt that some frightful hobgoblin had broken in upon them, and scampered away as fast as they could.

The coast now clear, our travelers soon sat down, and despatched what the robbers had left, with as much eagerness as if they had not expected to eat again for a month. As soon as they had satisfied themselves, they put out the lights, and each once more sought out a resting-place to his own liking. The donkey laid himself down upon a heap of straw in the yard; the dog stretched himself upon a mat behind the door; the cat rolled herself up on the hearth before the warm ashes; and the cock perched upon a beam on the top of the house; and as they were all rather tired with their journey, they soon fell asleep.

But about midnight, when the robbers saw from afar that the lights were out, and that all seemed quiet, they began to think that they had been in too great a hurry to run away; and one of them, who was bolder than the rest, went to see what was going on. Finding everything still, he marched into the kitchen, and groped about till he found a match in order to light a candle; and then espying the glittering, fiery eyes of the cat, he mistook them for live coals, and held the match to them to light it. But the cat, not understanding this joke, sprang at his face, and spit and scratched at him. This frightened him dreadfully, and away he ran to the back door; but there the dog jumped up and bit him in the leg; and as he was crossing the yard the donkey kicked him; and the cock, who had been awakened by the noise, crowed with all his might. At this the robber ran back as fast as he could to his comrades, and told the captain how a horrid witch had got into the house, and spat at him and scratched his face with her long bony fingers; how a man with a knife in his hand had hidden himself behind the door, and stabbed him in the leg; how a black monster stood in the yard and struck him with a club, and how a goblin sat upon the top of the house and cried out, "Throw the rascal up here!" After this the robbers never dared to go back to the house; but the musicians were so pleased with their quarters that they took up their abode there; and there they are, I dare say, at this very day.

THE STORY OF A CHICKEN

THERE was once a hen who had three chickens. The three chickens slept under her wing all night, and hopped about the yard all day. At the end of the yard there was a big door that shut the world out. The chickens were too small to see the top of the door, but they could peep underneath it, by bending their necks. The hen did not call her chickens by name, but by numbers. There was Number One, Number Two, and Number Three. Number One and Two were good, gentle, contented chickens that did not wish for more than they had got; but Number Three was not like them. He was tired of the yard, and of seeing nothing but the things there, and he wished to go into the world outside. At first he only began by wishing it a little, and then went on to wish it a great deal, till at last he wished it so much that he could not do without it. Instead of playing happily with his brothers on the steps in the yard, he went to the big door and stood looking at it, and sighing. One afternoon his mother found him there.

"What do you want?" said she.

"I want to get out," answered the chicken.

"Why?" said his mother.

"I don't know," answered the chicken; "but I want to get out."

99

The hen shook her head. "You're far better at home," said she. "It's no use wishing for it. Go and play on the steps with your brothers."

The chicken did so, because he had to obey. He tried to play happily like the others, but all the time he was thinking of the big door and the world that lay outside. When they went to bed under the hen's wing, he scarcely slept for thinking of it, or, if he slept at all, it was only to dream that he had gone. This went on for a week. After a week he could bear it no longer.

"To-day," he said, "when mother's sleeping, and Number One and Number Two are round the corner of the ash-hole, and can't see, I'll squeeze under the door and get out."

He did not tell this to anybody. After breakfast he played with the others, as usual. At last, his mother hung her head and shut her eyes and Number One and Number Two went to play beside the ash-hole. The time had come. The chicken ran to the big door very softly, looked round the yard with a beating heart, squeezed himself under it, and with a hard tug to get through, stood upright in the world outside. Oh, it was very delicious! The air of the world was so fresh, and there was so much of it, and there was no end to the things he saw, for at every step he saw something new.

"This is much nicer than the yard," said the chicken, drawing himself up. "This is really living!"

He walked along, looking about him. "It's not only wider," said he, "but higher. I'm sure it's higher than the yard. I can't see the top of it."

Presently he met an animal standing under a tree. He did not know its name, for he had never seen one like it before.

"Oh, big animal," said the chicken, boldly, "have you been in the world long?"

"Oh, little chicken!" said the animal, "yes."

"I've only just come in," said the chicken, "and I like it extremely. There's so much room."

"Room enough for you certainly," said the animal. "Where are you going?"

"How can you ask me," said the chicken, "when I tell you I've just come in?"

"I'll tell you then," said the animal, "go back home, don't go further."

"Everyone tells me that," said the chicken; "but I sha'n't. Our yard is so narrow—I can't stay in it."

"I advise you," said the animal, "to run back home; and I'm not only bigger than you, but wiser."

The chicken went on without minding him.

"Either I must be very small or something's very big," thought he. While he stared round him he forgot about the yard and his mother, and Number One and Number Two. The day passed without his noticing it; evening came on.

"I sha'n't be able to see much longer," said the chicken; "for it's getting dark. I must ask for something to eat. I feel hungry."

He was standing in the grass where a great number of families lived.

"Mr. Snail," said the chicken, "I'm hungry. Give me something to eat."

"I've nothing to give you," answered the snail. "It's not my business."

"But I'm hungry," said the chicken, feeling very uncomfortable. But the snail was gone.

The chicken walked on. He felt almost too hungry to look about him. Presently he saw a bird.

"Mr. Bird," he said, "I'm hungry. Give me something to eat."

The bird stared. "Why," he said, "you don't belong to me. It's not my business," and he flew away.

The chicken went on. The darkness was coming on. "How black it does get in the world!" said the poor little thing, shivering, "and how cold it is with nothing to warm one, to be sure!"

He stood still for he was too tired to walk on; besides, he had lost his way in the world. Presently a field mouse peeped out at him.

"I'm hungry!" called the chicken. "Do give me something to eat."

"Find something for yourself, you stupid bird!" said the field mouse, "it's not my business."

The poor little chicken now hung down its head. "The world must be very empty," said he, with a sigh, "if they can't spare me something out of it. I should have thought there would have been more than enough for everybody, but I suppose it's smaller than I thought."

Presently a grasshopper came up.

"I'm so hungry!" said the chicken. "Do give me something to eat."

"You must feed yourself, chicken," said the grasshopper. "I've got enough to feed at home. It isn't my business."

"I'll not ask any more," thought the poor little chicken, "for it's no use. I wish I was back in the yard. The world may be very big and grand to look at, but it's very uncomfortable to live in." And he hung his head again. He was so tired. Suddenly he felt himself laid hold of, and lifted up. He opened his eyes and saw a man. He had seen two men in his life before.

"I'm so hungry!" said the chicken, though he did not expect anything to come of it. "Will you give me something to eat?"

The man held him close to his warm hand, without answering, and the chicken stopped shivering.

"I shall soon be too hungry to speak!" thought he. They moved on silently. The chicken grew feebler and feebler. "I shall soon be too hungry to live!" thought he. At last the man stopped at the door out of the world, and the chicken roused himself. The man opened it, and went in. Then he bent down, and laid the chicken gently on the ground, and there stood his mother.

"Mother!" said the chicken, "I'm almost too hungry to live. There's nothing to eat outside in the world. Do give me something!"

The hen did so in a great hurry. She was delighted to see him.

"Number Three," she said, when he had quite finished, "come under my wing and rest. You must be very tired."

"Very," said the poor little chicken, creeping in. "How nice and warm it is, to be sure! It was so cold outside! Good-night, Mother."

And he fell fast asleep and never woke till morning.

FRISKIE'S NUTTING PARTY

Mr. Squirrel and his family had a pleasant home in a hollow tree. It was just the place, Mrs. Squirrel thought, for Friskie and Bushie and Graytail to have a good time. But Mr. Squirrel was not happy.

"I cannot find near enough nuts for us for the winter," Friskie heard him say to Mrs. Squirrel one morning.

"Did you gather them all from the large tree in the field?" Mamma Squirrel asked.

"Yes, but the boys had been there first and there were not many left."

"Dear me! Just think of Bushie and Friskie and Graytail perhaps hungry during the long, cold winter."

Friskie had heard it all and knew what made Papa Squirrel so sad. It was not long before Friskie was out in the field.

"I'm sure papa did not see the tree growing by the edge of the field, for not even the boys have found it out."

It was not such a long way from home and Friskie could go very fast.

Friskie was right. Neither the boys nor Papa Squirrel had found this tree, for the nuts lay scattered all over the ground. But how was he to carry them all home and store them away as a surprise for his papa as he had planned?

FRISKIE'S NUTTING PARTY

To be sure, Friskie had two tiny pockets, but what were they when there were so many nuts to be taken?

Friskie thought a while. It would be a good plan to pile them up in a small heap and bring Bushie and Graytail early in the morning to help. It wouldn't hurt if they did know the secret. Friskie knew they wouldn't tell.

The nuts made a large pile—large enough to make Papa Squirrel's heart leap with joy if he had seen them.

It was quite late when Friskie reached home. The sun had already sunk to rest and Bushie and Graytail were fast asleep.

"Never mind," thought Friskie, "we'll be up very early in the morning."

Friskie was tired, indeed, from his long journey and the sun had risen long before his eyes opened.

Bushie and Graytail were frisking on the branches when Friskie called them.

"We can have a nutting party to-day," he said. "It's quite a secret, for neither Papa nor Mamma Squirrel know anything about it."

When Friskie had finished telling all, both Bushie and Graytail were wild with joy.

"Come, we must start. It is late already."

Friskie led the way, telling them how hard they must work to have everything done by noon. They soon reached the tree.

"Here we are!"

Friskie made one bound and suddenly stopped. Not one nut was to be seen. Friskie was sure this was the place, he could tell just where the pile stood. What could have happened? No one could tell. It was plain to all that they must go home without one nut, and there was to be no surprise after all.

"What is the matter with you, Friskie and Bushie, and you, too, Graytail? You seem so unhappy," said Mr. Squirrel as they were eating their dinner.

"Surely you should be happier than usual to-day since Papa Squirrel found such a fine pile of nuts," said Mrs. Squirrel.

"Where did you find them?" asked Friskie anxiously.

"Under a tree not far away. I went out very early this morning and there I saw them all piled ready. I hurried back, and as you children were asleep, Mrs. Squirrel and I carried them home. Don't you think we should be happy with enough nuts for winter?"

Friskie could keep the secret no longer. Instead of the unhappy look a bright smile could be seen as he told the story.

"Well, Friskie, I am sorry I spoiled your nutting party, but you *did* help me a great deal after all."

THE DISCONTENTED WEATHERCOCK

ONCE upon a time there was a Weathercock which for many years had swung backwards and forwards on a tall pole near an old country house. At last it became very tired of telling the people which way the wind blew.

"What a miserable life I lead!" grumbled this Weathercock. "Creak-creak-creak! That is all I do, day and night! I never enjoy a moment's rest except when these good-for-nothing breezes take it into their heads to stop blowing for awhile. And they always make a point of taking their rest and exercise at such times as are least agreeable to me. I do believe that they change about to all points of the compass for no other reason than to tease and annoy me. It is too provoking. Last summer when I suffered intensely from the heat there was not the slightest puff of a breeze for days and days. Even an east wind would have been a real comfort to me, but not one stirred. And now, on New Year's Day, and for the past week I've been spun round and round so often that I'm too dizzy to see. Creak, creak, creak!"

At this moment two villagers who passed by gazed up at creaking Weathercock to see which way the wind blew.

"No one ever thinks how unpleasant it is to be perched up at the top of this pole. I'm quite sure that if I were loose I could fly as well as a bird," continued the Weathercock. "How I

108

should astonish the people! I'd fly over the treetops and to the point of the church steeple. I'm sure I should look far prettier than those dull-feathered winter birds. Their dark jackets cannot be compared in beauty to my gilded wings. When the sun strikes me on the top of this pole I am decidedly good-looking. But if I could flutter through the air I should be handsome indeed! Flying would be the easiest thing to do, if I were loose from this stupid pole!"

Here the Weathercock gave a stretch and a jerk. But instead of freeing itself, away it spun round and round as hard as it could go. After a while it became still again. Then it determined to hold itself perfectly stiff and not move one inch. It was hard to withstand the brisk gale which was blowing, but the Weathercock would not turn; it was thoroughly discontented with its work.

Now on washday when the people of the village saw that the Weathercock was standing still, they hung out their clothes to dry. To their surprise the high wind whisked them off the line and blew them all over the place.

The next day, to the great surprise of the Weathercock, one of the villagers brought a tall ladder, set it against the pole, and climbed to the top. He then poured so much oil around the Weathercock that it could not stand still for a moment; in fact, it began to shake and tremble like an aspen-leaf. The slightest puff of a breeze now turned the Weathercock. It continued, however, to grumble and fret, to twitch and jerk day after day.

"How I wish I could free myself and soar through the air!" it sighed again and again.

Suddenly, one day, a gust of wind whisked the Weathercock off the pole and up into the air.

"At last!" it exclaimed. "Here I go for the church steeple!"

But alas! its upward flight was very short. The next moment down it tumbled, clattering to the ground in a barnyard. And there it lay for hours half-choked among the straw and dirt. It could not stir, no matter how hard the wind blew.

And there among the rubbish of the barnyard the farmer found the Weathercock.

He kicked it and turned it over, saying: "Why, the poor old Weathercock has been blown down from the pole. We must see what the blacksmith can do to straighten it out. It is too bad that the pretty gilded wings are bent and blackened. It will never again be pretty to look at, but it will serve to show us which way the wind blows."

So he took the poor Weathercock to the blacksmith, who hammered it into shape on his anvil. The next day the farmer delighted the villagers by fastening the Weathercock at the top of its pole. And never again did it murmur or complain about showing the people which way the wind blew.

TEENCHY DUCK

ONCE upon a time there lived in a village in some country (I do not know where, but certainly nowhere near here), an old man and an old woman who were very poor indeed. They had never been able to save a single penny. They had no farm, not even a garden. They had nothing but a little duck that walked around on her two feet every day singing the song of famine. "Quack! quack! Who will give me a piece of bread? Quack! quack! Who will give me a piece of bread?" This little duck was so small that she was named Teenchy Duck.

It so happened one day that Teenchy Duck was paddling in the water near the river's edge when she saw a fine purse filled with gold. At once she began to flap her wings and cry: "Quack! quack! Who has lost his beautiful money?"

Just at that moment the Prince of the Seven Golden Cows passed along the road. He was richer than all the kings and emperors, but he was mean and miserly. He walked along with a stick in his hand, and as he walked he counted in his mind the millions that he had stored away in his strong-box.

"Quack! quack! Who lost his beautiful money? Quack! quack! Who lost his beautiful money?" cried Teenchy Duck.

"I have lost it," cried the Prince of the Seven Golden Cows, and then he seized the purse full of money that Teenchy Duck held in her bill, and went on his way.

The poor Puddle Duck was so astonished at this that she could scarcely stand on her feet.

"Well, well!" she exclaimed, "that rich lord has kept all for himself and given me nothing. May he be destroyed by a pestilence!"

Teenchy Duck at once ran to her master, and told him what had happened. When her master learned the value of what Teenchy Duck had found, and the trick that had been played on her by the Prince of the Seven Golden Cows, he went into a rage.

"Why, you big simpleton!" he exclaimed, "you find money and you do not bring it to us! You give it to a big lord, who did not lose it, when we poor people need it so much! Go out of this house instantly, and don't dare to come back until you have brought me the purse of gold!"

Poor Teenchy Duck trembled in all her limbs, and made herself small and humble; but she found her voice to say:

"You are right, my master! I go at once to find the Prince of the Seven Golden Cows."

But once out of doors, the poor Puddle Duck thought to herself sorrowfully: "How and where can I find the Prince who was so mean as to steal the beautiful money?"

Teenchy Duck was so bewildered that she began to strike her head against the rocks in despair. Suddenly an idea came into her mind. She would follow his tracks and the marks that his walking-stick made in the ground until she came to the castle of the Prince of the Seven Golden Cows.

The Sea Blossom

Page 77

The Goldfish

Page 139

TEENCHY DUCK

No sooner thought than done. Teenchy Duck went waddling down the road in the direction taken by the miserly Prince, crying with all her might:

"Quack! quack! Give me back my beautiful money! Quack! quack! Give me back my beautiful money!"

Brother Fox, who was taking his ease a little way from the road, heard Teenchy Duck's cries, and knew her voice. He went to her and said:

"What in the world is the matter with you, my poor Teenchy Duck? You look sad and broken-hearted."

"I have good reason to be," said Teenchy Duck. "This morning, while paddling in the river, I found a purse full of gold, and gave it to the Prince of the Seven Golden Cows, thinking it was his. But now, here comes my master and asks me for it, and says he will kill me if I do not bring it to him pretty soon."

"Well, where are you going in this style?" asked Brother Fox.

"I am going straight to the Prince of the Seven Golden Cows," said Teenchy Duck.

"Shall I go with you?" asked Brother Fox.

"I'd be only too glad if you would!" exclaimed Teenchy Duck.

"But how can I go?" said Brother Fox.

"Get into my satchel," said Teenchy Duck, "and I'll carry you the best I know how."

"It isn't big enough," said Brother Fox. "It will stretch," said Teenchy Duck. So Brother Fox got into the satchel, and Teenchy Duck went waddling along the road, crying: "Quack! quack! Give me back my beautiful money!"

She had not gone far when she met Brother Wolf, who was passing that way.

"What are you crying so for?" he inquired. "One would think you were going to die on the journey."

"It is only too true," said Teenchy Duck, and then she told Brother Wolf about finding the money purse, just as she had told Brother Fox.

"Perhaps I can be of some service to you," said Brother Wolf. "Shall I go with you?"

"I am willing," said Teenchy Duck.

"But how can I go so far?" Brother Wolf asked.

"Get into my satchel," said Teenchy Duck, "and I'll carry you as best I can."

"It is too small," said Brother Wolf.

"It will stretch mightily," said Teenchy Duck.

So Brother Wolf also got into the satchel with Brother Fox.

Teenchy went on her way again. She didn't walk very fast, for her satchel was heavy; but she never ceased crying: "Quack! quack! Give me back my beautiful money."

Now it happened, as she was going along, she came up with a Ladder, which said, without asking after her health:

"My poor Teenchy Duck! You do not seem to be very happy."

"I should think not!" exclaimed Teenchy Duck.

"What can the matter be?" the Ladder asked.

Teenchy Duck then told her story over again.

"I am not doing anything at present," said the Ladder, "shall I go with you?"

"Yes," said Teenchy Duck.

"But how can I go, I who never walk?" inquired the Ladder.

"Why, get into my satchel," said Teenchy Duck, "and I'll carry you the best I know how."

The Ladder was soon in the satchel with Brother Fox and Brother Wolf, and Teenchy Duck went on her way, following the tracks of the Prince of the Seven Golden Cows, and always crying: "Quack, quack! Give me back my beautiful money!"

Going along and crying thus, Teenchy Duck came to her best and oldest friend, the River.

"What are you doing here?" said the River, in astonishment, "and why are you crying so? When I saw you this morning you seemed very happy."

"Ah!" said Teenchy Duck, "would you believe it? I have not eaten since yesterday."

"And why not?" asked the sympathetic River.

"You saw me find the purse of gold," said Teenchy Duck, "and you saw the Prince seize it. Ah, well! my master will kill me if I do not get it and return it to him."

"Sometimes," the River replied, "a little help does a great deal of good. Shall I go with you?"

"I should be very happy," said Teenchy Duck.

"But how can I follow you—I that have no limbs?" said the River.

"Get into my satchel," said Teenchy Duck. "I'll carry you as best I can."

Then the River got into the satchel by the side of the other friends of Teenchy Duck.

She went on her journey, keeping her eyes on the ground, so as not to lose sight of the tracks of the thief, but still crying for her beautiful money. On her way she came to a Bee-Hive, which had a mind to laugh because Teenchy Duck was carrying such a burden.

"Hey, my poor Teenchy Duck," said the Bee-Hive.

"I'm not in the humor for joking, my dear," said Teenchy Duck.

"Why are you so sad?"

"I have been very unfortunate, good little people," said Teenchy Duck, addressing herself to the Bees, and then she told her story.

"Shall we go with you?" asked the Bees.

"Yes, yes!" exclaimed Teenchy Duck. "In these days of sorrow I stand in need of friends."

"How shall we follow you?" asked the Bees.

"Get into my satchel," said Teenchy Duck. "I'll carry you the best I know how."

Then the Bees shook their wings for joy and swarmed into the satchel along with the other friends of Teenchy Duck.

She went on her way always crying for the return of her beautiful money. She walked and walked without stopping to rest a moment, until her legs almost refused to carry her. At last, just as night was coming on, Teenchy Duck saw with joy that the tracks of the Prince of the Seven Golden Cows stopped at the iron gate that barred the way to a splendid castle.

"Ah!" she exclaimed, "I have arrived at my journey's end, and I have no need to knock on the gate. I will creep under."

TEENCHY DUCK

Teenchy Duck entered the grounds and cried out: "Quack! quack! Give me back my beautiful money!"

The Prince heard her and laughed scornfully. How could a poor Teenchy Duck compel a great lord to return the purse of gold?

Teenchy Duck continued to cry:

"Quack! quack! Give me back my beautiful money."

It was night, and the Prince of the Seven Golden Cows ordered one of the servants to take Teenchy Duck and shut her up in the hennery with the turkeys, the geese, and the chickens, thinking that these fowls would kill the stranger, and that her disagreeable song would forever be at an end.

This order was immediately carried out by the servant, but no sooner had Teenchy Duck entered the hennery than she exclaimed:

"Brother Fox, if you do not come to my aid, I am lost."

Brother Fox came out of the satchel promptly, and worked so well at his trade that of all the fowls he found there, not one remained alive.

At break of day the servant-girl, whose business it was to attend to the poultry-yard, opened the door of the hennery, and was astonished to see Teenchy Duck come out, singing the same old song: "Quack! quack! Give me back my beautiful money!"

The astonished girl immediately told her master, the Prince, what had happened, and the wife of the Prince, who had at that moment learned all, said to her husband:

"This duck is a witch. Give her the money, or it will bring us bad luck."

The Prince of the Seven Golden Cows refused to listen. He believed that the fox had only happened to enter his hennery by accident.

Teenchy Duck made herself heard all day, and at night the Prince said to his servants:

"Take this squaller and throw her into the stable under the feet of the mules and horses. We will see in the morning what she will say."

The servants obeyed, and Teenchy Duck immediately cried:

"Brother Wolf, if you do not come quickly to my aid I shall be killed."

Brother Wolf made no delay, and it was not long before he had destroyed the horses and the mules. Next morning, before day, the servants went to get the animals to put them to the ploughs and wagons; but when they saw them lying dead their astonishment was great. In the stable Teenchy Duck stood alone, singing in her most beautiful voice:

"Quack! quack! Give me back my beautiful money!"

When the Prince of the Seven Golden Cows heard the sad news, he became white with rage, and in his fury he wanted to give his servants a thousand lashes for not having taken better care of the animals. But his wife calmed him a little, saying:

"My husband, give back to Teenchy Duck this purse you have taken, or else we shall be ruined."

"No," cried the Prince, "she shall never have it!"

All this time Teenchy Duck was walking up and down, to the right and to the left, singing at the top of her voice:

"Quack! quack! Give me back my beautiful money!"

"Heavens!" said the Prince, stopping his ears, "I am tired of hearing this ugly fowl squall and squawk. Quick! throw her into the well or the furnace, so that we may be rid of her."

"What shall we do first?" the servants asked.

"It matters not," said the Prince, "so long as we are rid of her."

The servants took Teenchy Duck and threw her into the well, thinking this the easier and the quicker way to be rid of her.

As Teenchy Duck was falling, she cried: "Come to my assistance, good Ladder, or I am undone."

The Ladder immediately came out of the satchel, and leaned against the walls of the well. Teenchy Duck came up the rounds, singing:

"Quack! quack! Give me back my beautiful money!"

Everybody was astonished, and the Prince's wife kept saying: "Give the witch her money."

"They would say that I am afraid of a Teenchy Duck," said the Prince of the Seven Golden Cows. "I will never give it up." Then, speaking to his servants, he said: "Heat the oven! Heat it to a white heat, and throw this witch in."

The servants had to obey, but they were so frightened that none dared touch her. At last, one bolder than the rest seized her by the end of the wing and threw her into the red-hot oven. Everybody thought that this was the end of Teenchy Duck, but she had had time to cry out:

"Oh! my dear friend River, come to my assistance, or I shall be roasted!"

The River rushed out and quenched the fire and cooled the oven.

When the Prince went to see what was left of Teenchy Duck, she met him and began to repeat her familiar song:

"Quack! quack! Give me back my beautiful money!"

The Prince of the Seven Golden Cows was furious.

"You are all blockheads!" he cried to his servants. "You never knew how to do anything. Get out of here! I will drive you off the place. Hereafter I will take charge of this witch myself."

That night, before retiring, the Prince and his wife went and got Teenchy Duck, and prepared to give her such a beating as they had no doubt would cause her death.

Fortunately, Teenchy Duck saw the danger and cried out:

"Friend Bees, come out and help me!"

A buzzing sound was heard, and then the Bees swarmed on the Prince and his wife, and stung them so badly they became frightful to behold.

"Return the money to this ugly witch," groaned the unfortunate wife. "Run, or we are done for."

The Prince did not wait to be told twice. He ran and got the purse of gold, and returned it to Teenchy Duck.

"Here," said he, "I am conquered. But get out of my grounds quickly."

Full of joy, Teenchy Duck went out into the road, singing: "Quack! quack! I have got my beautiful money! Quack! quack! Here is my beautiful money!"

On her way home she returned the friends that had aided her

to the places where she had found them, thanking them kindly for their help in time of need.

At break of day Teenchy Duck found herself at her master's door. She aroused him by her loud cries. After that, the family was rich and Teenchy Duck was well taken care of. If she went to the village pond it was only to tell her comrades of her remarkable way of gaining the beautiful money.

FINDING A DARK PLACE

THEY were all talking about a dark place, a *very* dark place where there was no ray of light.

The tiny brown bird turned her head on one side and said, "I shall go and see it." Away she flew. In a short time she came back.

"Is it a very dark place?" asked the bee.

"Oh, yes," nodded the bird. "It *is* a very dark place."

"I shall go and see for myself," buzzed the bee.

"Buzz, buzz, buzz." The bee was gone a long time but at last he came back.

"What did you find?" asked a big butterfly.

"I found the dark place," buzzed the bee. "It was the darkest place I ever saw. I shall not go near it again."

"Oh, I must see it!" said the butterfly.

It took the butterfly several hours to find the place. But at last he found it. When he came back he said to the bee, and the bird, "What a dark place it is—I never saw anything like it."

"Puff! Puff! Puff!" said the wind. "I, too, want to peep into that dark place you are all talking about. Puff! Puff! Puff!"

He puffed out his cheeks and blew himself along as fast as he could. When he came back he was almost out of breath but he managed to say, "A dark place! A dark, dark place! Black as night! Black as night!"

"Is it, indeed?" said the sun. "Well, I must go and see about it." He was gone a whole day. The brown bird, the bee, the butterfly, and the wind were all waiting for him when at last he came back.

"Did you see it?" they all asked together.

"I couldn't find a dark place anywhere," said the sun. "I've searched all day long and I couldn't find this dark place you are all talking about."

"I wonder why he couldn't find it," said the others to themselves.

Can you tell why?

MR. MOON HIDES

"WHAT'S the matter? asked the Earth.

"I'm tired," said the Moon.

"All right," said the Earth. "My shadow is always ready for you to hide behind when you want it."

"You don't mind, do you?" asked the Moon.

"I'm highly flattered," said the Earth. "It is a great honor. Lots of people come out and look at us both at such times. For people call it an Eclipse."

"What do they mean by that?" asked the Moon.

"They call it a total eclipse," said the Earth, "when there is no Moon to be seen at all."

"My! And they use words like that—total Eclipse—just to say that the Moon can't be seen. Well, well, well, they do pay me a great compliment."

The Moon talked to the Earth for a long time and the Earth's shawl or shadow kept the moon from sight for several hours.

Before long the Moon grew a little restless. "I think I must be leaving," he said.

"Sorry to see you go," said the Earth. "You call on me so seldom. Your visits are so rare."

"Oh," laughed the Moon, "you are so nice to me, but where did you pick up that last word? Was it running around down on the earth where you heard it as it walked over you?"

"Words don't run around," said the Earth, "but the people who use them do. That word means that your visits are so few. I'd like to see you oftener."

"Thank you," said the Moon. "Perhaps because I come only now and again it is better, for you see it is more of a treat."

"Maybe that is so," said the Earth. "I always enjoy looking at you from afar, but I do thoroughly enjoy your calls."

"Then I'll come some time again," said the Moon.

THE CIRCUS DREAM

"I WANT to tell you the story this evening," said daddy, "of a little boy named Jay Rial.

"Jay Rial was as nice a little boy as any one could ever hope to see. Everyone liked him and he liked people, too. But the thing he loved above everything else in the world was the circus.

"He loved the sound of the train whistle which brought the circus to town, and he loved the old circus which used to travel by the road and not come by the train at all. He loved the circus band, the clowns, the animals. He loved the very tent itself, the smell of peanuts, the roars of the lions, the beautiful ladies who rode the beautiful horses.

"He loved the performers, and every time he went to a circus he wished his eyes were bigger so he could see more, and he wished that circus people didn't have to go to sleep at all.

"He used to follow the circus parade as it came through the town and he didn't mind if it was always late, for he could go to the circus grounds with some of the other boys and see them unpack, and maybe he could sometimes help a little, too!

"Once he had been allowed to stand in the middle of the sawdust-covered ring when they were fixing up the tent. That had been a great moment.

126

THE CIRCUS DREAM

"There was only one thing about circus day which ever made him sad. That was that sometimes people couldn't afford to go to the circus. He had been very lucky. He was always able to do chores for his mother and daddy around circus time and he could make enough money for a ticket.

"But there were some little boys and girls who couldn't do that, or whose mothers and daddies couldn't afford to do that for them.

"'If I ever get to be a big man,' said little Jay Rial, 'I'm going to take just as many children to the circus with me as I can.'

"Little Jay Rial called it his circus-dream. And sometimes he would really dream that he was taking hundreds and hundreds of little boys and girls whose faces had been sad and teary because they hadn't thought they were going to the circus. He had dreamed of how they would follow after him and would say:

"'Me, too?'

"And he would smile at them and say, 'Yes, all of you!'

"It was a beautiful dream.

"Now there are many people who dream of doing something fine when they have more money or when they're grown up and who forget it when that time comes.

"They will excuse themselves by saying, 'Yes, I have more money than I used to have, but I find I need it all,' instead of doing more than they had been able to do before. There are little boys who say, 'When I grow up I'm going to see that poor children get ice-cream once in a while.' But when they grow up they forget and they don't realize that there are lots of children in hospitals and in homes who very seldom receive visits from the ice-cream man.

"Now Jay Rial was different. He remembered. When he grew up he went into the circus business. He was the one who would tell the newspapers in the different towns in advance when the circus was coming to town so every one could look forward to it.

"And he remembered his circus dream.

"So every year when the circus came to the very biggest city they visited, grown up Jay Rial arranged that every child in every hospital or home or any child who was crippled or not as fortunate as other children should come to the circus free.

"They arranged one afternoon when no one need buy a ticket but when every seat was free. And yet, that wasn't enough for Jay Rial. When the hospitals and homes sent in their lists of the numbers of children who would be able to go to the circus the lists grew so long that the place wouldn't hold them all.

"Do you suppose Jay Rial said, 'Sorry, but we've room for no more?' Not a bit of it. He had another circus party for those who couldn't come to the first. And Jay Rial's face was full of smiles as he looked at the thousands of children who were shrieking with joy over the circus, and he said, 'My dream has come true.'

"But," ended daddy, "Jay Rial is one of those people who help to make dreams come true."

THE FISHERMAN AND HIS WIFE

THERE was once a fisherman who lived with his wife in a ditch, close by the sea-side. The fisherman used to go out all day long a-fishing; and one day, as he sat on the shore with his rod, looking at the shining water and watching his line, all on a sudden his float was dragged away deep under the sea: and in drawing it up he pulled a great fish out of the water. The fish said to him, "Pray let me live: I am not a real fish; I am an enchanted prince, put me into the water again, and let me go." "Oh!" said the man, "you need not make so many words about the matter; I wish to have nothing to do with a fish that can talk; so swim away as soon as you please." Then he put him back into the water, and the fish darted straight down to the bottom, and left a long streak of blood behind him.

When the fisherman went home to his wife in the ditch, he told her how he had caught a great fish, and how it had told him it was an enchanted prince, and that on hearing it speak he had let it go again. "Did you not ask it for anything?" said the wife. "No," said the man, "what should I ask for?" "Ah!" said the wife, "we live very wretchedly here in this nasty stinking ditch; do go back, and tell the fish we want a little cottage."

The fisherman did not much like the business: however, he

went to the sea, and when he came there the water looked all yellow and green. And he stood at the water's edge, and said,

> "O man of the sea!
> Come listen to me,
> For Alice my wife,
> The plague of my life,
> Hath sent me to beg a boon of thee!"

Then the fish came swimming to him, and said, "Well, what does she want?" "Ah!" answered the fisherman, "my wife says that when I had caught you, I ought to have asked you for something before I let you go again; she does not like living any longer in the ditch, and wants a little cottage." "Go home, then," said the fish, "she is in the cottage already." So the man went home, and saw his wife standing at the door of a cottage. "Come in, come in," said she; "is not this much better than the ditch?" And there was a parlour, and a bed-chamber, and a kitchen; and behind the cottage there was a little garden with all sorts of flowers and fruits, and a court-yard full of ducks and chickens. "Ah!" said the fisherman, "how happily we shall live!" "We will try to do so at least," said his wife.

Everything went right for a week or two, and then Dame Alice said, "Husband, there is not room enough in this cottage, the court-yard and garden are a great deal too small; I should like to have a large stone castle to live in; so go to the fish again, and tell him to give us a castle." "Wife," said the fisherman, "I don't like to go to him again, for perhaps he will be angry; we ought to be content with the cottage." "Nonsense!" said the wife; "he will do it very willingly; go along, and try."

The fisherman went; but his heart was very heavy: and when he came to the sea, it looked blue and gloomy, though it was quite calm, and he went close to it, and said,

"O man of the sea!
Come listen to me,
For Alice my wife,
The plague of my life,
Hath sent me to beg a boon of thee!"

"Well, what does she want now?" said the fish. "Ah!" said the man very sorrowfully, "my wife wants to live in a stone castle." "Go home then," said the fish, "she is standing at the door of it already." So away went the fisherman, and found his wife standing before a great castle. "See," said she, "is not this grand?" With that they went into the castle together, and found a great many servants there, and the rooms all richly furnished and full of golden chairs and tables; and behind the castle was a garden, and a wood half a mile long, full of sheep, and goats, and hares, and deer; and in the court-yard were stables and cow-houses. "Well," said the man, "now will we live contented and happy in this beautiful castle for the rest of our lives." "Perhaps we may," said the wife; "but let us consider and sleep upon it before we make up our minds": so they went to bed.

THE FISHERMAN AND HIS WIFE

The next morning, when Dame Alice awoke, it was broad day-light, and she jogged the fisherman with her elbow, and said, "Get up, husband, and bestir yourself, for we must be king of all the land." "Wife, wife," said the man, "why should we wish to be king? I will not be king." "Then I will," said Alice. "But, wife," answered the fisherman, "how can you be king? the fish cannot make you a king." "Husband," said she, "say no more about it, but go and try; I will be king!" So the man went away, quite sorrowful to think that his wife should want to be king. The sea looked a dark grey color, and was covered with foam as he cried out,

> "O man of the sea!
> Come listen to me,
> For Alice my wife,
> The plague of my life,
> Hath sent me to beg a boon of thee!"

"Well, what would she have now?" said the fish. "Alas!" said the man, "my wife wants to be king." "Go home," said the fish; "she is king already."

Then the fisherman went home; and as he came close to the palace, he saw a troop of soldiers, and heard the sound of drums and trumpets; and when he entered in, he saw his wife sitting on a high throne of gold and diamonds, with a golden crown upon her head; and on each side of her stood six beautiful maidens, each a head taller than the other. "Well, wife," said the fisherman, "are you king?" "Yes," said she, "I am king." And when he had looked at her for a long time, he said, "Ah, wife! what a fine thing it is to be king! now we shall never have anything more to wish for." "I don't know how that may be," said she; "never is a long time. I am king, 'tis true, but I begin to be tired of it, and I think I should like to be emperor." "Alas, wife! why should you wish to be emperor?" "Husband," said she, "go to the fish; I say I will be emperor." "Ah, wife!" replied the fisherman, "the fish cannot make an emperor, and I should not like to ask for such a thing." "I am king," said Alice, "and you are my slave, so go directly!" So the fisherman was obliged to go; and he muttered as he went along, "This will come to no good, it is too much to ask, the fish will be tired at last, and then we shall repent of what we have done." He soon arrived at the sea, and the water was quite black and muddy, and a mighty whirlwind blew over it; but he went to the shore, and said,

"O man of the sea!
Come listen to me,
For Alice my wife,
The plague of my life,
Hath sent me to beg a boon of thee!"

"What would she have now?" said the fish. "Ah!" said the fisherman, "she wants to be emperor." "Go home," said the fish; "she is emperor already."

So he went home again; and as he came near he saw his wife sitting on a very lofty throne made of solid gold, with a great crown on her head full two yards high, and on each side of her stood her guards and attendants in a row, each one smaller than the other, from the tallest giant down to a little dwarf no bigger than my finger. And before her stood princes, and dukes, and earls: and the fisherman went up to her, and said, "Wife, are you emperor?" "Yes," said she, "I am emperor." "Ah!" said the man as he gazed upon her, "what a fine thing it is to be emperor!" "Husband," said she, "why should we stay at being emperor; I will be pope next." "O wife, wife!" said he, "how can you be pope? there is but one pope at a time in Christendom." "Husband," said she,"I will be pope this very day." "But," replied the husband, "the fish cannot make you pope." "What nonsense!" said she, "if he can make an emperor, he can make a pope, go and try him." So the fisherman went. But when he came to the shore the wind was raging, and the sea was tossed up and down like boiling water, and the ships were in the greatest distress and danced upon the waves most fearfully; in the middle of the sky was a little blue, but towards the south it was all red as if a dreadful storm was rising. At this the fisherman was terribly frightened, and trembled, so that his knees knocked together: but he went to the shore and said,

"O man of the sea!
Come listen to me,
For Alice my wife,
The plague of my life,
Hath sent me to beg a boon of thee!"

THE FISHERMAN AND HIS WIFE

"What does she want now?" said the fish. "Ah!" said the fisherman, "my wife wants to be pope." "Go home," said the fish, "she is pope already."

Then the fisherman went home, and found his wife sitting on a throne that was two miles high; and she had three great crowns on her head, and around stood all the pomp and power of the Church; and on each side were two rows of burning lights, of all sizes, the greatest as large as the highest and biggest tower in the world, and the least no larger than a small rush-light. "Wife," said the fisherman as he looked at all this grandeur, "are you pope?" "Yes," said she, "I am pope."

"Well, wife," replied he, "it is a grand thing to be pope; and now you must be content, for you can be nothing greater." "I will consider of that," said the wife. Then they went to bed: but Dame Alice could not sleep all night for thinking what she should be next. At last morning came, and the sun rose. "Ha!" thought she as she looked at it through the window, "cannot I prevent the sun rising?" At this she was very angry, and she wakened her husband, and said, "Husband, go to the fish and tell him I want to be lord of the sun and moon." The fisherman was half asleep, but the thought frightened him so much, that he started and fell out of bed. "Alas, wife!" said he, "cannot you be content to be pope?" "No," said she, "I am very uneasy, and cannot bear to see the sun and moon rise without my leave. Go to the fish directly."

Then the man went trembling for fear; and as he was going down to the shore a dreadful storm arose, so that the trees and rocks shook; and the heavens became black, and the lightning played, and the thunder rolled; and you might have seen in the sea great black waves like mountains with a white crown of foam upon them; and the fisherman said,

"O man of the sea!
Come listen to me,
For Alice my wife,
The plague of my life,
Hath sent me to beg a boon of thee!"

"What does she want now?" said the fish. "Ah!" said he, "she wants to be lord of the sun and moon." "Go home," said the fish, "to your ditch again!" And there they live to this very day.

Tales and Legends
Beautiful

THE GOLDFISH

FREDDIE had gone with Mother to visit Aunt Delia and was having a very happy time. He had been driving behind the fat white pony, and he had played with the little black dog, Beauty, until he was quite tired out. So he snuggled down among the gay silk cushions on the window seat and lay sleepily watching the goldfish above him. For of all the lovely things in Aunt Delia's home, the goldfish, swimming forever around and around in the big glass globe, were the most wonderful to Freddie. Although he was such a little boy, he had gone fishing with Father a number of times but had never seen any fish like these. As he lay watching them he wondered if they were real, live, slippery fish like those Father caught, or if they were made of gold and were wound up like his toy engine.

The more he watched them spinning around, the more curious he became until at last he stood up on the window seat, put one little fat hand on the globe to steady it and, dipping the other in the water, tried to catch one of the fish. Oh, yes, they were certainly alive! They darted hither and thither, growing more and more frightened as Freddie splashed the water around them. Suddenly he was very much surprised to hear a queer, gasping voice say:

"Oh, little boy, why do you frighten us so?"

Freddie's hand came slowly out of the water.

THE GOLDFISH

"Because I want to know if you are gold or slippery," he said.

"Both," answered the fish.

"Why?" asked Freddie.

"Shall I tell you?" said the little fish.

"Yes," answered Freddie. So the goldfish began:

"Once, a long time ago, a star fell from out the blue sky, down to earth and splashed into a lake of clear water. Then the fish in the lake heard a wonderful, sweet voice calling them, so they all came up to the surface and saw a tall, white angel who seemed to be clothed in fleecy clouds. His face was sad and he said:

" 'Little fish, I have lost one of my bright stars from heaven. Can you find it for me?'

"Then the little fish, and there were many kinds of them in the lake, began to swim hither and thither, looking for the lost star. But by and by they came up to the top of the water and said to the angel:

" 'We cannot find your star. It is lost.'

" 'It cannot be lost,' said the angel. 'It must be found, for not one star can be spared from the sky. Will you not look again for it?'

"But the little fish were tired and swam away—all but one, the smallest of them all.

" 'I will look again, oh, beautiful angel,' he said.

"And, after a long time, he came back and in his mouth was the lost star. As the angel stooped to take it, his face was bright as the sun, and he said lovingly to the little fish:

THE GOLDFISH

" 'For this you shall always wear a golden coat. Be good and happy, and I will protect you.'

"And ever since then, my brothers and I have worn these gold coats, and we try to be good and happy."

Just then Mother came into the room.

"Freddie," she cried, "are you frightening Aunt Delia's goldfish?"

"No, Mother," answered the child, "and I never will any more, for I know how they got their gold coats."

INSIDE THE GARDEN GATE

ONCE, long, long ago, when the silver moon was shining up in the sky, and the small golden stars were twinkling, a little fairy with a bundle of dreams went hurrying home to fairyland.

She looked up at the stars and moon to see what time it was, for the fairy queen had bidden her come back before the day dawned.

"I shall not be late," said the fairy, as she flew like a thistle-down through the air or tripped over the heads of the flowers; but in her haste, she flew into a spider's web, which held her so fast that, although she struggled again and again, she could not get free.

Her bundle of dreams fell out of her arms, and lay on the ground; and the poor little fairy burst into tears, for she knew that that daylight always spoiled dreams, and these were lovely ones.

Her shining wings were tangled in the web, her hands were chained, and her feet were helpless; so she had to lie still and wait for the daytime, which, after all, came too soon.

As soon as the sun was up, Mrs. Spider came out of her den; and when she saw the fairy she was very glad, for she thought she had caught a new kind of fly.

"If you please, Mrs. Spider, I am only a little fairy, and flew into your web last night on my way home to fairyland."

"A fairy!" said Mrs. Spider crossly, for she was disappointed.

"I suppose you are the one who helps the flies to get away from me. You see well enough then!"

"I help them because they are in trouble," answered the fairy gently.

"So are you, now," snapped the spider. "But the flies won't help you."

"But perhaps you will," pleaded the fairy.

"Perhaps I won't," said the spider, going back into her house and leaving the little fairy, who felt very sorrowful.

Her tears fell like dewdrops on the spider's web, and the sun shone on them, and made them as bright as the fairy queen's diamonds.

The fairy began to think of the queen and the court, and the bundle of dreams; and she wondered who would do the work if she never got free. The fairy queen had always trusted her, and had sent her on many errands.

Once she had been sent to free a mockingbird that had been shut in a cage. She remembered how he sang in his cage, although he was longing for his green tree-tops.

She smiled through her tears when she thought of this and said to herself:

"I can be singing, too! It is better than crying."

Then she began to sing one of her fairy songs:

> "Oh! listen well, and I will tell,
> Of the land where the fairies dwell;
> The lily bells ring clear and sweet
> And green grass grows beneath your feet
> In the land where the fairies dwell,
> In the land where the fairies dwell."

Now, though the fairy did not know it, Mrs. Spider was very fond of music; and when she heard the sweet song she came out to listen. The little fairy did not see her, so she sang on.

"There's love, sweet love, for one and all—
    For love is best for great and small—
    In the land where the fairies dwell,
    In the land where the fairies dwell."

Just as the fairy finished the song she looked up, and there was Mrs. Spider, who had come out in a hurry.

"The flies are not going to help you," said she, "so I will," and she showed the fairy how to break the slender thread, until she was untangled and could fly away through the sunshine.

"What can I do for you, dear Mrs. Spider?" the fairy asked, as she picked up her bundle of dreams.

"Sing me a song sometimes," replied Mrs. Spider. But the fairy did more than that; for soon after she reached fairyland, the fairy queen needed some lace to wear on her dress at a grand ball.

"Fly into the world," she said, "and find me a spinner; and tell her that when she has spun the lace she may come to the ball, and sit at the queen's table."

As soon as the fairy heard this, she thought of the spider and made haste to find her and tell her the queen's message.

"Will there be music?" asked the spider.

"The sweetest ever heard," answered the fairy; and the spider began to spin.

The lace was so lovely, when it was finished, that the fairy queen made the spider court spinner; and then the spider heard the fairies sing every day, and she too had love in her heart.

(*Slightly abridged.*)

144

WHAT YOU LOOK FOR YOU WILL FIND

THERE was once a queen who was very unhappy because her ladies and gentlemen were always quarreling. Every day they came to her with very unpleasant stories about one another. At last she called a secret council of her wise men and asked them how she could prevent this.

Some of the wise men advised severe punishment. Others thought that the discontented courtiers should be sent away. At last one old man with snowy white hair stepped forward and said:

"O Queen, live forever! Your lords and ladies are like naughty children. They are jealous of one another; so they are always trying to find one another's faults. Can you not in some way teach them how wicked such feelings are? If you can, they may be ashamed and may do better."

The queen listened and was pleased. She dismissed her wise men, and sent for her lords and ladies. When all had come, she said:

"I am going to send two pages out on errands in which you will all be interested. I have called you together to see them start; and when they come back, I will call you together again to see what news they bring. Call the first page."

145

WHAT YOU LOOK FOR YOU WILL FIND

When the page stood before her, she said:

"I wish you to mount a trusty horse and ride through all my kingdom. Visit all the gardens on your way around the kingdom, and bring me the most beautiful flowers that you can find. You may start out by taking the road to the right."

The page bowed and was gone; and a moment later they heard his horse's hoofs on the pavement.

"Call the other page," said the queen.

When the other page stood before her, she said to him:

"I wish you to mount a trusty horse and ride through all my kingdom. Visit all the gardens on your way around my kingdom and bring me the most bitter and harmful weeds that you can find. You may start out by taking the road to the left."

This page also bowed and was gone.

The queen did not explain why she sent these pages on errands so strange. She merely said that they would all meet again when the pages returned.

Several days passed. At last the queen was told that both pages had returned. She then sent for her lords and ladies.

When all were assembled the queen said:

"Admit the first page."

A moment later he entered, and his arms were filled with lovely flowers. These he laid at the queen's feet.

"Well," said the queen, "what did you find?"

"O Queen," said the page, "your kingdom is a kingdom of flowers. I never knew before that there were so many beautiful flowers."

"Were there no weeds?" asked the queen.

"There may have been, but I did not see them."

So she dismissed this page and ordered the next to be admitted.

And when the second page entered his arms were filled with bitter and harmful weeds. Some of them were so poisonous that he had to wear thick gloves to protect his hands.

"And what did you find?" asked the queen.

"O Queen," he said, "your kingdom is filled with weeds. I did not imagine there could be so many different kinds, or such poisonous ones."

"But did you see no flowers?"

"There may have been flowers," said the page, "but I did not see them, of course there must have been some, but I was looking for weeds and did not notice the flowers."

When the second page was gone, the queen looked at her lords and ladies. They hung their heads in shame. She had intended to make a little speech, urging them to look for flowers instead of weeds in one another's lives. But they seemed to understand; so she said nothing.

And after that she did not hear any more complaining and the unhappy quarreling ceased.

THE WATER LILY

THERE was once a little boy who was very fond of pictures. There were not many pictures for him to look at, for he lived long ago near a great American forest. His father and mother had come from England, but his father was dead now. His mother was very poor, but there were still a few beautiful pictures on the walls of her house.

The little boy liked to copy these pictures; but as he was not fond of work, he often threw his drawings away, before they were half done. He said that he wished that some good fairy would finish them for him.

"Child," said his mother, "I don't believe that there are any fairies. I never saw one—and your father never saw one. Anyway, if there are fairies, they are jealous and unkind. Mind your books, my child, and never mind the fairies."

"Very well, Mother," said the boy.

"It makes me sad to see you stand looking at the pictures," said his mother another day, as she laid her hand on his curly head. "Why, child, pictures can't feed a body, pictures can't clothe a body, and a log of wood is far better to burn and warm a body."

"All that is quite true, Mother," said the boy.

"Then why do you keep looking at them, child?"

148

But the boy could only say, "I don't know, Mother."

"You don't know! Nor I, neither! Why, child, you look at the dumb things as if you loved them! Put on your cap and run out to play."

So the boy wandered off into the forest till he came to the brink of a little sheet of water. It was too small to be called a lake; but it was deep and clear, and was overhung with tall trees. It was evening and the sun was getting low.

The boy stood still beside the water and thought how beautiful it was to see the sun, red and glorious, between the black trunks of the pine trees. Then he looked up at the great blue sky and thought how beautiful it was to see the little clouds folding over one another like a belt of rose-coloured waves. Then he looked at the lake and saw the clouds and the sky and the trees all reflected there, down among the lilies.

And he wished that he were a painter, for he said to himself, "I am sure there are no trees in the world with such beautiful leaves as these pines. I am sure there are no clouds in the world so lovely as these. I know this is the prettiest little lake in the world, and if I could paint it, everyone else would know it, too."

But he had nothing to paint with. So he picked a lily and sat down with it in his hand and tried very hard to make a correct drawing of it. But he could not make a very good picture. At last he threw down his drawing and said to the lily:

"You are too beautiful to draw with a pencil. How I wish I were a painter!"

As he said these words he felt the flower move. He looked, and the cluster of stamens at the bottom of the lily-cup glittered

149

like a crown of gold. The dewdrops which hung upon the stamens
changed to diamonds before his eyes. The white petals flowed together and the next moment a beautiful little fairy stood on his
hand. She was no taller than the lily from which she came, and
she was dressed in a robe of the purest white.

"Child, are you happy?" she asked.

"No," said the boy in a low voice, "because I want to paint
and I cannot."

"How do you know that you cannot?" asked the fairy.

"Oh, I have tried a great many times. It is of no use to try
any more."

"But I will help you."

"Oh," said the boy. "Then I might succeed."

"I heard your wish, and I am willing to help you," said the
fairy. "I know a charm which will give you success. But you
must do exactly as I tell you. Do you promise to obey?"

"Spirit of a water-lily!" said the boy. "I promise with all my
heart."

"Go home, then," said the fairy, "and you will find a little
key on the doorstep. Take it up."

"I will," said the boy. "What shall I do then?"

"Carry the key to the nearest pine tree," said the fairy, "strike
the trunk with it, and a keyhole will appear. Do not be afraid
to unlock your door. Slip in your hand, and you will bring out
a magic palette. You must be very careful to paint with colours
from that palette every day. On this depends the success of the
charm. You will find that it will make your pictures beautiful
and full of grace.

"If you do not break the spell, I promise you that in a few years you shall be able to paint this lily so well that you will be satisfied; and that you shall become a truly great painter."

"Can it be possible?" said the boy. And the hand on which the fairy stood trembled for joy.

"It shall be so, if only you do not break the charm," said the fairy. "But lest you forget what you owe to me, and as you grow older even begin to doubt that you have ever seen me, the lily you gathered to-day will never fade till my promise is fulfilled."

The boy raised his eyes and when he looked again there was nothing in his hand but the flower.

He arose with the lily in his hand, and went home at once. There on the doorstep was the little key, and in the pine tree he found the magic palette. He was so delighted with it and so afraid that he might break the spell that he began to work that very night. After that he spent nearly all his time working with the magic palette. He often passed whole days beside the sheet of water in the forest. He painted it when the sun shone on it and it was spotted all over with the reflections of fleeting white clouds. He painted it covered with water lilies rocking on the ripples. He painted it by moonlight, when but two or three stars in the empty sky shone down upon it; and at sunset, when it lay trembling like liquid gold.

But the fairy never came back to look at his work. He often called to her when he had been very successful. But she never made any answer.

So the years passed, and the boy grew to be a man. He had

never broken the charm. The lily had never faded, and he still worked every day with his magic palette.

But no one cared for his pictures. Even his mother did not like them. His forests and misty hills and common clouds were too much like the real ones. She said she could see as good any day by looking out of her window. All this made the young man very unhappy. He began to doubt whether he should ever be a painter, and one day he threw down his palette. He thought the fairy had deserted him.

He threw himself on his bed. It grew dark, and he soon fell asleep; but in the middle of the night he awoke with a start. His chamber was full of light, and his fairy friend stood near the lily.

"Shall I take back my gift?" she asked.

"Oh, no, no, no!" cried he. He was rested now and he did not feel so much discouraged.

"If you still wish to go on working, take this ring," said the fairy. "My sister sends it to you. Wear it, and it will greatly assist the charm."

He took the ring, and the fairy was gone. The ring was set with a beautiful blue stone, which reflected everything bright that came near it; and he thought he saw inside the ring the one word —"Hope."

Many more years passed. The young man's mother died, and he went far, far from home. In the strange land to which he went people thought his pictures were wonderful; and he had become a great and famous painter.

One day he went to see a large collection of pictures in a great city. He saw many of his own pictures, and some of them had been painted before he left his forest home. All the people and the painters praised them; but there was one that they liked better than the others. It was a picture of a little child, holding in its hands several water lilies.

Toward evening, the people departed one by one, till he was left alone with his masterpieces. He was sitting in a chair thinking of leaving the place, when he suddenly fell asleep. And he dreamed that he was again standing near the little lake in his native land, watching the rays of the setting sun as they melted away from its surface. The beautiful lily was in his hand and while he looked at it the leaves became withered, and fell at his feet. Then he felt a light touch on his hand. He looked up, and there on the chair beside him stood the little fairy.

"O wonderful fairy!" he cried, "how can I thank you for your magic gift? I can give you nothing but my thanks. But at least tell me your name so that I may cut it on a ring and always wear it."

"My name," replied the fairy, "is *Perseverance.*"

THE IMPRISONED NIXIE

Now it happened that the water was very crystal clear in a river which flowed between tall sedges and forget-me-nots, like angel's eyes. The river was so clear because it was the home of a very beautiful Water Nixie who lived in it, and who sometimes could emerge from her home and sit in woman's form upon the bank. She had a dark green smock upon her, the colour of the water-weed that waves as the water wills it, deep, deep down. And in her long, wet hair were the white flowers of the water-violet, and she held a reed mace in her hand. Her face was very sad, because she had lived a long life, and known so many adventures, ever since she was a baby, which was nearly a hundred years ago.

For creatures of the streams and trees live a long, long time, and when they die they lose themselves in Nature. That means that they are forever clouds, or trees, or rivers, and never have the form of men and women again.

All water creatures would live, if they might choose it, in the sea, where they are born. It is in the sea they float hand-in-hand upon the crested billows, and sink deep in the great troughs of the strong waves, that are green as jade. They follow the foam and lose themselves in the wide ocean,—

THE IMPRISONED NIXIE

Where great whales come sailing by,
Sail and sail with unshut eye;
And they store in the Sea King's palace
The golden phosphor of the sea.

But this Water Nixie had lost her happiness through not being good. She had forgotten many things that had been told her, and she had done many things that grieved others. She had stolen some one else's property—quite a large bundle of happiness—which belonged elsewhere and not to her. Happiness is generally made to fit the person who owns it, just as do your shoes, or clothes; so that when you take some one's else, it's very little good to you, for it fits badly, and you can never forget that it isn't yours.

So what with one thing and another, this Water Nixie had to be punished, and the Queen of the Sea had banished her from the waves.

The punishment that can most affect Merfolk is to restrict freedom. And this is how the Queen of the Sea punished the Nixie of our tale.

"You shall live for a long time in little places, where you will weary of yourself. You will learn to know yourself so well that everything you want will seem too good for you, and you will cease to claim it. And so, in time, you shall get free."

Then the Nixie had to rise up and go away, and be shut into the fastness of a very small space, according to the words of the Queen. And this small space was—a tear.

At first she could hardly express her misery, and by thinking

155

so continuously of the wideness and savour of the sea, she brought a dash of the brine with her, that makes the saltness of our tears. She became many times smaller than her own stature; even then, by standing upright and spreading wide her arms, she touched with her finger-tips the walls of her tiny crystal home. How she longed that this tear might be wept, and the walls of her prison shattered! But the owner of this tear was of a very proud nature, and she was so sad that tears seemed to her in no wise to express her grief.

She was a Princess who lived in a country that was not her home. What were tears to her? If she could have stood on the top of the very highest hill and with both hands caught the great winds of heaven, strong as they, and striven with them, perhaps she might have felt as if she expressed all she knew. Or, if she could have torn down the stars from the heavens, or cast her mantle over the sun. But tears! Would they have helped to tell her sorrow? You cry if you spoil your copybook, don't you—or pinch your hand? So you may imagine the Nixie's home was a safe one, and she turned round and round in the captivity of that tear.

For twenty years she dwelt in that strong heart, till she grew to be accustomed to her cell. At last, in this wise came her release.

An old gypsy came one morning to the castle and begged to see the Princess. She must see her, she cried. And the Princess came down the steps to meet her, and the gypsy gave her a small roll of paper in her hand. And the roll of paper smelt like honey as she took it, and it adhered to her palm as she opened it. There was a little sign of writing on the paper, but in the midst of the page was a picture, small as the picture reflected in the iris of an eye. The picture showed a hill, with one tree on the sky-line, and a long road wound round the hill.

And suddenly in the Princess' memory a voice spoke to her. Many sounds she heard, gathered up into one great silence, like the quiet there is in forest spaces, when it is summer and the green is deep:

"Blessed are they that have the home longing,
    For they shall go home."

Then the Princess gave the gypsy two golden pieces, and went up to her chamber, and long that night she sat, looking out upon the sky.

She had no need to look at the honeyed scroll, though she held it closely. Clearly before her did she see that small picture: the hill, and the tree, and the winding road, imaged as if mirrored in the iris of an eye. And in her memory she was upon that road, and the hill rose beside her, and the little tree was outlined, every twig of it, against the sky.

And as she saw all this, an overwhelming love of the place arose in her, a love of that certain bit of country that was so sharp and strong, that it stung and swayed her, as she leaned on the window-sill.

And because the love of a country is one of the deepest loves you may feel, the band of her control was loosened, and the tears came welling to her eyes. Up they brimmed and over in salty rush and follow, dimming her eyes, magnifying everything, speared for a moment on her eyelashes, then shimmering to their fall. And at last came the tear that held the disobedient Nixie.

Splash! it fell. And she was free.

If you could have seen how pretty she looked standing there, about the height of a grass-blade, wringing out her long, wet hair! Every bit of moisture she wrung out of it, she was so glad to be quit of that tear. Then she raised her two arms above her in one delicious stretch, and if you had been the size of a mustard-seed perhaps you might have heard her laughing. Then she grew a little, and grew and grew, till she was about the height of a blue-bell, and as slender to see.

She stood looking at the splash on the window-sill that had been her prison so long, and then, with three steps of her bare feet she reached the jessamine that was growing by the window, and by this she swung herself to the ground.

Away she sped over the dew-drenched meadows till she came to the running brook, and with all her longing in her outstretched hands, she kneeled down by the crooked willows among all the comfry and the loosestrife, and the yellow irises and the reeds.

Then she slid into the wide, cool stream.

CHILD CHARITY

ONCE upon a time there lived in the west country a little girl who had neither father nor mother; they both died when she was very young, and left her to the care of her uncle, who was the richest farmer in all that country.

He had houses and lands, flocks and herds, with many servants to work about his house and fields. He also had a very rich wife and two fair daughters.

The father and mother were as proud as peacocks, the daughters thought themselves the greatest beauties in the world and not one of the family would speak a kind word to anybody they thought beneath them.

Now the little orphan girl was not like this. She was kind to everyone. The poorer they were, the more ready was she to help them. That was why the people of the west country called her Child Charity and if she had any other name, I never heard it.

Child Charity was thought very little of in that proud house. Her uncle would not own her for his niece; her cousins would not keep her company; and her aunt sent her to work in the dairy, and to sleep in the back garret where they kept all sorts of lumber and dry herbs for the winter.

All the day she cleaned pails, scrubbed floors, and washed dishes; but every night she slept in the back garret as sound as a princess could in her palace.

159

CHILD CHARITY

One day they were making merry in the house, when a poor old woman came to the back door begging for food and a night's rest. Her clothes were coarse and ragged; her hair was thin and gray; her back was bent; her teeth were gone. In short, she was the poorest old woman that ever came begging.

The first who saw her was the kitchen-maid, and she told her to be gone. The next was the cow-boy, and he threw her a bone over his shoulder; but Child Charity, hearing the noise, came out from her seat at the foot of the lowest table, and asked the old woman to take her share of the supper, and sleep that night in her bed in the back garret. The old woman sat down without a word of thanks.

All the company laughed at Child Charity for giving her bed and her supper to a beggar, but she did not mind. She scraped the pots for her supper that night and slept on a sack, while the old woman rested in her warm bed; and next morning, before the little girl awoke, she was up and gone, without so much as saying thank you or good-morning.

The next day at supper-time, who should come to the back-door but the old woman, again asking for food and a night's rest. No one would listen to her or give her a crumb, till Child Charity rose from her seat at the foot of the lowest table, and kindly asked her to take her supper, and sleep in her bed in the back garret.

Again the old woman sat down without a word. Again Child Charity scraped the pots for her supper and slept on the sack. In the morning the old woman was gone; but for six nights after, as sure as the supper was spread, there was she at the back-door, and the little girl always asked her in.

160

CHILD CHARITY

Child Charity's aunt said she would let her get enough of beggars. Her cousins made fun of her and her visitor. Sometimes the old woman said, "Child, why don't you make this bed softer— and why are your blankets so thin?" but she never gave her a word of thanks nor a civil good-morning.

At last, on the ninth night from her first coming, when Child Charity was getting used to scraping the pots and sleeping on the sack, her usual knock came at the door, and there she stood with an ugly, gray dog, so stupid-looking and clumsy that no herdboy would keep him.

"Good-evening, my little girl," she said when Child Charity opened the door. "I will not have your supper and bed to-night —I am going on a long journey to see a friend; but there is a dog of mine, whom nobody in all the west country will keep for me.

"He is a little cross, and not very handsome; but I leave him to your care till the shortest day in all the year. Then you and I will count for his keeping."

When the old woman had said the last word, she set off with such speed that Child Charity lost sight of her in a minute. The ugly dog began to fawn upon her, but he snarled at everyone else. The servants said he was a disgrace to the house. The proud cousins wanted him drowned, and it was with great trouble that Child Charity got leave to keep him in an old cow-house.

Ugly and cross as the dog was, he fawned on her, and the old woman had left him to her care. So the little girl gave him part of all her meals, and, when the hard frost came, took him to her own back garret, because the cow-house was damp and cold in the long nights. The dog lay quietly on some straw in a corner.

Child Charity slept soundly, but every morning the servants would say to her:

"What great light and fine talking was that in your back garret?"

"There was no light but the moon shining in through the window, and no talk that I heard," said Child Charity, and she thought they must have been dreaming. But night after night, when any of them awoke in the dark and silent hour that comes before the morning, they saw a light brighter and clearer than the Christmas fire, and heard voices like those of lords and ladies in the back garret.

Partly from fear and partly from laziness none of the servants would rise to see what might be there; till at length, when the winter nights were at the longest, the little parlour-maid, who did least work and got most praise because she took tales to her mistress, crept out of bed when all the rest were sleeping, and set herself to watch at a crack of the door.

At first the maid saw nothing but the dog lying quietly in the corner, Child Charity sleeping soundly in her bed, and the moon shining through the window; but an hour before daybreak there came a glare of lights and a sound of far-off bugles.

The window opened and in marched a troop of little men clothed in crimson and gold, and bearing every man a torch, till the room looked bright as day. They marched up and bowed to the dog where he lay on the straw and the most richly clothed among them said:

"Royal Prince, we have prepared the dining-hall. What will Your Highness please that we do next?"

"Ye have done well," said the dog. "Now prepare the feast for the princess and I mean to bring a stranger who never feasted in our halls before."

"Your Highness' commands shall be obeyed," said the little man, making another bow; and he and his company passed out of the window. By and by there was another glare of lights and a sound like far-off flutes.

The window opened, and there came in a company of little ladies dressed in pink velvet, and carrying each a glass lamp. They also walked up to the dog, and, bowing, said:

"Royal Prince, what will Your Highness please that we do?"

"Prepare the robes," said the dog, "for the princess and I will bring with us a stranger who never feasted in our halls before."

"Your Highness' commands shall be obeyed," said the little lady, making a low curtsey; and she and her company passed out through the window, which closed quietly behind them. The dog stretched himself out upon the straw, the little girl turned in her sleep, and the moon shone in on the back garret.

The parlour-maid was so much amazed, and so eager to tell this great story to her mistress, that she could not close her eyes that night, and was up before cock-crow; but when she told it, her mistress called her a silly girl to have such foolish dreams, and scolded her so that the parlour-maid dared not mention what she had seen to the servants.

But Child Charity's aunt thought there might be something in it worth knowing; so next night, when all the house were asleep, she crept out of bed, and set herself to watch at the back garret door.

CHILD CHARITY

There she saw exactly what the maid told her—the little men with the torches and the little ladies with the glass lamps, come in bowing to the dog, and the same words pass; only he said to the one, "Now prepare the presents," and to the other, "Prepare the jewels;" and when they were gone the dog stretched himself on the straw, Child Charity turned in her sleep, and the moon shone in on the back garret.

The mistress could not close her eyes any more than the maid from eagerness to tell the story. She woke Child Charity's rich uncle before cock-crow; but when he heard it, he laughed at her for a foolish woman, and told her not to repeat it before the neighbours, lest they should think she had lost her senses.

The mistress could say no more, and the day passed; but that night the master thought he would like to see what went on in the back garret; so when all the house were asleep he slipped out of bed and set himself to watch at the crack in the door.

The same thing happened again that the maid and the mistress saw—the little men in crimson with their torches, and the little ladies in pink velvet with their lamps, came in at the window, and made a low bow to the ugly dog.

The one said: "Royal Prince, we have prepared the presents," and the other, "Royal Prince, we have prepared the jewels;" and the dog said to them all:

"Ye have done well. To-morrow come and meet me and the princess with horses and chariots, for we will bring a stranger from this house who has never traveled with us, nor feasted in our halls before."

CHILD CHARITY

The little men and the little ladies said, "Your Highness' commands shall be obeyed." When they had gone out through the window, the ugly dog stretched himself out on the straw, Child Charity turned in her sleep, and the moon shone in on the back garret.

The master could not close his eyes any more than the maid or the mistress, for thinking of this strange sight. He remembered to have heard his grandfather say that somewhere near his meadows there lay a path leading to the fairies' country, and the hay-makers used to see it shining through the gray summer morning as the fairy bands went home.

Nobody had heard or seen the like for many years; but the master felt sure that the doings in his back garret must be fairy work, and the ugly dog a person of great account. His chief wonder was, however, what visitor the fairies meant to take from his house, and after thinking the matter over, he was sure it must be one of his daughters—they were so handsome and had such fine clothes.

So the first thing Child Charity's rich uncle did that morning was to get ready a breakfast of roast mutton for the ugly dog, and carry it to him in the old cow-house; but not a morsel would the dog taste. He barked at the master, and would have bitten him if he had not run away with his mutton.

"The fairies have strange ways," said the master to himself, but he called his daughters to him and told them to dress themselves in their best, for he could not say which of them might be called into great company before night. Child Charity's proud cousins, hearing this, put on the richest of their silks and laces, and waited for the call their father spoke of, while the little girl scoured and scrubbed in the dairy.

They were in very bad temper when night fell and nobody had come; but just as the family were sitting down to supper the ugly dog began to bark, and the old woman's knock was heard at the back door. Child Charity opened it, and was going to offer her bed and supper as usual, when the old woman said:

"This is the shortest day in all the year, and I am going home to hold a feast after my travels. I see you have taken good care of my dog, and now if you will come with me to my house, he and I will do our best to entertain you. Here is our company."

As the old woman spoke there was a sound of far-off flutes and bugles, then a glare of lights; and a great company, dressed so grandly that they shone with gold and jewels, came in open chariots, covered with gilding and drawn by snow-white horses. The first and finest of the chariots was empty. The old woman led Child Charity to it by the hand, and the ugly dog jumped in before her.

The proud cousins, in their fine dresses, had by this time come to the door, but nobody wanted them; and no sooner were the old woman and her dog within the chariot than a great change passed over them.

The ugly woman turned at once to a beautiful young princess, with long yellow curls and a robe of green and gold; while the ugly dog at her side started up a fair young prince, with nut-brown hair and a robe of purple and silver.

"We are," said they, as the chariots drove on, and the little girl sat astonished, "a prince and princess of Fairyland, and we wanted to find out whether or not there were good people still to be found in these false and greedy times."

Some of the farmer's household, who were looking after them through the moonlight night, said the chariots had gone one way across the meadows, some said they had gone another, and till this day they cannot agree upon the way.

But Child Charity went with that noble company into a country such as she had never seen—for primroses covered the ground, and the light was always like that of a summer evening. They took her to a royal palace, where there was nothing but feasting and dancing for seven days. She had robes of pale green velvet to wear, and slept in a lovely room.

When the feast was done, the prince and princess gave her such heaps of gold and jewels that she could not carry them, but they gave her a chariot to go home in, drawn by six white horses; and on the seventh night, when the farmer's family had settled in their own minds that she would never come back, and were sitting down to supper, they heard the sound of her coachman's bugle, and saw her alight with all the jewels and gold at the very back-door where she had brought in the ugly old woman. The fairy chariot drove away and never came back to that farmhouse after.

But Child Charity scrubbed and scoured no more, for she grew a great lady, even in the eyes of her proud cousins.

LITTLE GOPOLA

LITTLE GOPOLA lived with his mother in a cottage near a great forest. His father was dead and he and his mother were very, very poor. But kind neighbours helped them to dig the ground and plant the seed so that they always had enough to eat.

When the time came for little Gopola to go to school he needed new clothes and the poor mother had hard work to earn enough money to buy them for him. But at last all was ready, and one bright morning Gopola's mother blessed her little son as she stood in the door and watched him make his way to the path which led through the forest to the village. Gopola had never been through the great forest alone and the way seemed very long and very lonely. But as soon as he caught sight of the village school his heart leaped with joy as he hastened to join the other children.

It was a happy day for the little child. He lingered a long time at the schoolmaster's house; and, when at last he did set out to go home, it was almost dark. Again he had to go through the forest alone and he became so frightened that he ran as fast as his little legs would carry him.

"Gopola, Gopola!" he heard his mother's voice calling through the darkness, and the next moment he was safe at home in her arms.

LITTLE GOPOLA

Gopola did not wish to go to school after that and his mother could not understand why.

"You had such a happy day, Gopola. Why do you not wish to go to school again?"

"I am afraid to go alone through the forest, dear Mother," replied the child.

The good mother felt very sorry that she was too poor to send anyone through the forest with Gopola and she could not leave her work to go with him herself. But suddenly, she thought of the Divine Child Krishna,* who sometimes appeared as a child and sometimes as a humble cowherd boy, and she said, "Gopola, never be afraid to come from school again. You have a little cowherd brother who lives in the forest. He is never far from the path. If you will call out to him, 'Oh, cowherd brother, come and walk through the forest with me,' he will be sure to come and then you will not be afraid."

"Is it really true that my brother will come and take care of me?" asked the child.

"Yes, it is true—just as true as it is that you are God's child and that He loves you," said his mother.

Gopola was now no longer afraid and he started off bravely. The next morning when he reached the forest path he called out, "Oh, cowherd brother, come and play with me."

No sooner had he called than the bushes parted and out stepped a child with a gold crown upon his head. He took Gopola by the hand and together they ran and played all the way through the forest.

At night Gopola found the little cowherd brother waiting for

*Krishna is a popular deity in the Hindu religion.

him and again they ran and played together all the way home. And every morning and night the little child—always with the gold crown upon his head—was waiting patiently for little Gopola who was now no longer afraid. He told his mother of the happy times he had with his little brother and she knew He was the Divine Child Krishna who loved all little children and was ever ready to help and comfort them.

One day the schoolmaster told the children that he was going to give a party. It was the custom in that country for the children to bring gifts of food and clothing to their schoolmaster; so as soon as it became known, the children went home to their parents and asked what gifts they could bring. When Gopola told his mother about the party, she was very sad because she was too poor to give her child any gift for his master. Again she thought of the Divine Krishna. Then with a cheerful smile she said, "Gopola, I have nothing for you to give; but when you see your little brother again, tell Him about it and ask Him to help you."

The next morning Gopola and the Child played all the way to school. When they reached the edge of the forest Gopola said: "O little cowherd brother, our teacher is going to give a party to-day, and I have nothing to give him. Can you help me?"

"I am but a poor cowherd, Gopola. What can I give him? Oh, I know——" and away ran the little cowherd to the forest. In a moment he returned carrying a small bowl full of curds.

"This is all I have, Gopola," he said. "Take it and give it to your teacher."

Gopola thought it a fine present and hastened to carry it to his master's house. But the poor child's little gift was not noticed among the many lovely presents brought by the other children and Gopola felt very unhappy. Tears came into his eyes. Just then the master caught sight of Gopola standing near with the bowl of curds for him. He thanked the child, then took the bowl from him and emptied the curds into a larger bowl. But to his wonder the small bowl was at once full of curds again. Once more the master emptied the curds into the larger bowl, but again the small bowl was full. And the master kept on, but the small bowl filled faster than he could empty it; so that every child had some of the curds and still there was much to spare.

"What does this mean?" they asked. "Where did you get this bowl of curds?"

"My little cowherd brother gave it to me," answered Gopola, reverently, for now he understood that his little companion of the forest was no other than the Divine Child of whom his mother had so often told him.

"Who is he?" asked the schoolmaster, kindly.

"One who wears a crown on his head. He comes and plays with me on my way to school and home again."

"I wish you would take me to your little brother," said the master. So, hand-in-hand, Gopola and the master made their way to the edge of the forest. But the little cowherd brother did not come as He had always done to meet Gopola.

"Little cowherd brother! Little cowherd brother! Come!" called the child. But there was no answer. Gopola did not know what to do. He saw a stern look come into the master's face and he feared that the master would think he had not told the truth. So he called out once more with all the voice he had, "O, cowherd brother, please come. If you do not they will think I do not tell the truth."

"Nay, little brother, I cannot show My face. Thy master has long to wait before he can see Me. Few children, indeed, are blessed with mothers like thine."

THE BANYAN DEER

ONCE upon a time in a far country there lived a king who was very fond of hunting the wild deer. Each day many of the men who belonged to the working people were forced to go with the king on his hunting trips. This took many hours of the poor people's time, so one day they met together to see what could be done to free them from giving so much time to the king's sport.

One of the old men said: "Let us drive large herds of deer into the king's great park. We will plant food for them and see that there is a supply of fresh water. Then the king can hunt without our help."

So they planted plenty of grass in the royal park and walled in with rocks the clear water from many springs. Then they drove into the enclosure two great herds of deer, the Banyan herd and the Velvet herd. Now it happened that the leaders of these herds were stags of wondrous beauty. They had the softest skin which was the colour of burnished gold, their round eyes sparkled like precious gems, their silvery horns gleamed in the sunlight, and their hoofs were as fine and hard as polished ebony.

When the two herds were safely enclosed in the royal park the people went to the king and said, "O King, we have driven many deer into the royal forest, where you may now hunt without our help. We beg you to let us go on with our own work."

The king was well pleased and agreed to grant the men's request. The next morning His Majesty went to the enclosed

THE BANYAN DEER

woodland to see the herds. He was so surprised and pleased with the beauty of the leaders that he said:

"King of the Banyan deer and king of the Velvet herd, your lives shall be spared."

Each day, however, one of the other animals was killed for the king's dinner. Sometimes the royal cook would shoot the quarry and sometimes the king himself would kill one of the timid creatures. The poor animals soon learned to know what the king or his cook wanted when either of them came to the forest. As soon as the deer caught sight of the bow and arrows away through the forest they sped, trembling with fear.

One day the leader of the Banyan deer went to the leader of the Velvet deer and said: "My friend, let us plan a way to relieve the suffering of our creatures. Since we know the king's will is to kill off all in the herds, let the deer take death by turns. One day the lot shall fall to one of my herd; the next day, to one of yours. In this way much suffering will be spared, since the others may live in peace until their time to die comes."

The Velvet deer agreed to this plan and each day by lot one deer was killed for the king.

One day it happened that the lot fell to a mother deer, in the Velvet herd. Her little one was very young and helpless so she went to the leader and said, "O King of the herd, I come to ask if my life may be spared a little longer. Without a mother's care my little one will die. Spare me until he is stronger, then I'll willingly give up my life."

But the king of the Velvet herd said, "Nothing can be done for you. It is your turn to die."

Sadly she turned away and sought the king of the Banyan deer. When he had heard her story he said, "Your life shall be spared. Go in peace."

The mother deer hastened back to her fawn and the king of the Banyan herd went to offer his own life in her place.

When the king saw the beautiful leader of the Banyan herd waiting to be killed His Majesty said, "What does this mean? Did I not promise to spare your life? Why are you lying here?"

And the beautiful Banyan leader said, "O King, the lot fell to a mother deer whose helpless little one would die without her care. She begged me to spare her life until her fawn is a little older. I cannot ask another in the herd to take her place so I have come to give up my life for her."

"Arise, O king of the Banyan deer," said His Majesty. "Arise and go in peace. For your loving kindness I grant you your life and also the mother deer hers."

The Banyan deer rose and said, "O King, life is sweet to all in the herds."

And the king answered, "Life shall be spared to all. Say to all the deer in the herds that they are free."

"Life is sweet to all creatures in the forest, O King," said the Banyan deer.

And the king said, "Life is sweet to all. Go in peace and tell the creatures of the forest they shall not be killed to satisfy the king's selfish pleasure."

So through his great unselfishness the Banyan deer brought the blessing of life to all the creatures of the forest.

THE COUNTRY OF MICE

Once upon a time the king of a large country was sitting in his Great Hall. A servant entered and said, "O King, a queer little mouse dressed in royal robes begs to see you. He says he is king of the country of mice."

The king laughed and said, "He may enter."

The page held the door of the Great Hall open and the mouse in royal robes walked slowly toward the king's throne.

"You are welcome, Brother Mouse," said the king. "How can I serve you?"

"O King," replied the mouse, "the crops were very poor this year. My subjects will starve unless we can borrow enough grain for the winter. Therefore I, King of the Mice, have come here to ask if Your Majesty can help us. If you will lend us grain we will serve you faithfully and repay you at the next harvest."

"Tell me how much grain you need," said the king.

"I think we shall need one of your big barns full," answered the tiny visitor.

"But if I should let you have such a large amount, how could you carry it away?" asked the king in surprise.

"Leave that to me, Sire," said the mouse. "If you will let us have the grain, we'll carry it away."

"King of the Mice, I will let you have one of my great barns full of barley. You may come for the grain whenever you wish."

"Your Majesty, I thank you with all my heart," said the mouse, bowing deeply. Then he turned and slowly walked out of the Great Hall.

That night the King of the Mice called his subjects together and told them to empty one of the great barns which belonged to the neighbouring king. Many hundreds of mice went together and each one picked up as much grain as he could carry in his mouth, on his back, and curled up in his tail.

The next morning the king went out to look at his barn. He laughed when he saw that the mice had not left a single grain of barley.

After the next harvest the King of the Mice sent back the amount of barley which he had borrowed and also a fine present for the king who had been kind in a time of need.

Now it happened shortly after this that the King of the Mice came to the Great Hall to see his friendly neighbour.

The king of the country was very busy, but he gave word that he would spare a few moments for his little royal friend.

Slowly the King of the Mice walked up the Great Hall. Making a deep bow, he said, "Your Majesty, this time I've come to offer help, not to ask for it."

"To offer help, Brother Mouse?" said the king in surprise. "Tell me what you mean."

"The last time I was here, O King, you did me and my people a great favour. Now I've come to offer you our help."

The great king smiled and said, "Pardon me, sir, but I do not see how you can help. An enemy has declared war on my kingdom and an army much larger than mine is gathering across the river which borders my country."

"O King," answered the Mouse, "the last time I was here you did not think my people could carry away the grain you lent us. But we did so. All we ask now is that you will trust us when we say that we can help you."

The king was very much surprised by the mouse's speech.

"You kept your word before, Brother Mouse," he said; "therefore, I am willing to trust you. Tell me how I can help you in this plan."

"This is what we wish to do, O King," answered the mouse. "To-morrow evening give us one hundred thousand sticks, each about a foot long. Have them laid in rows on the bank of the river."

"What you ask shall be done," said the king.

"And we will save your kingdom, Sire," said the Mouse, bowing deeply before he left the Great Hall.

The next evening the King of the Mice led two hundred thousand of his people down to the edge of the river. There he found the sticks laid out ready for them. Two mice jumped on each of the sticks, pushed off from the bank, and sailed across the river to the enemy's camp.

It was very dark and the soldiers were all asleep. Some of them lay in tents and others were stretched out in the open air. Their war arms lay beside them ready for use.

At a sign from their king, all the mice scampered silently through the camp, and began to carry out the orders they had received. Some nibbled at the bowstrings; others gnawed the clothes or bit off the pigtails of the sleeping men. In two hours they nibbled into shreds the arms, tents, and stores of the enemy. Then, silently as they came, the army of mice gathered together on the bank of the river and sailed quietly over to their own shore.

The next morning at daybreak a great outcry broke from the soldiers' camp. Each man as he rose from his sleep found his clothes in rags, his pigtail cut off, his bow without a string, and the food for breakfast gone. The soldiers were very much frightened.

Suddenly from the opposite bank they heard the sound of bugles. They cried out, "We cannot give battle. Let us flee for our lives."

Away they fled in all directions, and in a few moments not a man was to be seen.

The king of the country soon learned why his enemies had taken flight. He sent for the King of the Mice in order to thank him for saving the country.

"How shall we prove to you that we are truly grateful, Brother Mouse?" asked the king.

"There are two dangers, Sire, which always threaten my people," said the Mouse. "You see, our homes are burrows in the lowlands near the river. Whenever the water rises a little it overflows the country and floods our nests."

"That danger I can easily overcome," said the king of the country. "A strong embankment shall be built. This will keep the water from overflowing into your nests. Tell me how I can serve you further."

"Thank you, Sire—our other danger is cats," said the Mouse.

"Cats!" cried the king. "To be sure! I hereby banish all cats from my kingdom. Also, I forbid any of my subjects on pain of death to keep a cat."

The King of the Mice bowed deeply and said, "Again, O King, I thank you. If we are no longer worried by floods and cats we shall live happily and safely. Farewell."

"One word more, Brother Mouse," said the king. "I hereby order that each year the gift of a barnful of grain be taken to you and your people for the help which you gave me in time of trouble."

"Again I thank you," said the King of the Mice.

Then he hurried away to tell his people the good news of the reward they had earned because they served the king of the country in a time of need.

LITTLE DAYLIGHT

ONCE upon a time a beautiful little princess, named Daylight, was born in a far-away country. All the fairies in the land were invited to her christening, and an old witch who was not invited was there, too. The fairies knew she was there for no good, and they planned to keep her from doing as much evil as they could.

Five fairies had one after the other given the child such gifts as each counted best, and the fifth had just stepped back to her place, when, mumbling a laugh between her toothless gums, the wicked witch hobbled out into the middle of the circle, and at the moment when the archbishop was handing the baby to the lady at the head of the nursery department, addressed him thus, giving a bite or two to every word before she could part with it:

"Please your grace, I'm very deaf; would your grace mind repeating the princess's name?"

"With pleasure, my good woman," said the archbishop, stooping to shout in her ear; "the infant's name is Little Daylight."

"And Little Daylight it shall be," cried the fairy, in the tone of a dry axle, "and little good shall any of her gifts do her. For I bestow upon her the gift of sleeping all the day long, whether she will or not. Ha, ha! He, he! Hi, hi!"

Then out started the sixth fairy, who, of course, the others had arranged should come after the wicked one, in order to undo as much as she might.

181

"If she sleeps all day," she said, mournfully, "she shall at least wake all night."

"You spoke before I had done," said the wicked fairy.

"That's against the law. It gives me another chance."

"I beg your pardon," said the other fairies, all together.

"She did. I hadn't done laughing," said the crone.

"I had only got to Hi, hi! and I had to go through Ho, ho! and Hu, hu! So I decree that if she wakes all night she shall wax and wane with its mistress, the moon. And what that may mean I hope her royal parents will live to see. Ho, ho! Hu, hu!"

But out stepped another fairy, for they had been wise enough to keep two in reserve, because every fairy knew the trick of one.

"Until," said the seventh fairy, "a prince comes who shall kiss her without knowing it."

The wicked fairy made a horrid noise like an angry cat and hobbled away. She could not pretend that she had not finished her speech this time, for she had laughed Ho, ho! and Hu, hu!

"I don't know what that means," said the poor king to the seventh fairy.

"Don't be afraid. The meaning will come with the thing itself," said she.

I will not attempt to describe what they had to go through for some time. For at certain seasons the palace rang all night with bursts of laughter from Little Daylight, whose heart the old fairy's curse could not reach; she was Daylight still, only a little in the wrong place, for she always dropped asleep at the first hint of dawn in the east. But her merriment was of short duration.

When the moon was at the full, she was in glorious spirits, and

as beautiful as it was possible for a child of her age to be. But
as the moon waned, she faded, until at last she was wan and withered like the poorest, sickliest child you might come upon in the
streets of a great city in the arms of a homeless mother. Then
the night was quiet as the day, for the little creature lay in her
gorgeous cradle night and day with hardly a motion, and indeed,
at last without even a moan, like one dead.

At first they often thought she was dead, but at last they got
used to it, and only consulted the almanac to find the moment
when she would begin to revive, which, of course, was with the
first appearance of the silver thread of the crescent moon. Then
she would move her lips, and they would give her a little food;
and she would grow better and better and better, until for a few
days she was splendidly well. When well, she was always merriest out in the moonlight; and even when near her worst, she
seemed better when, in the warm summer nights, they carried
her cradle out into the light of the waning moon. Then in her
sleep she would smile the faintest, most pitiful smile.

For a long time very few people ever saw her awake. As she
grew older she became such a favourite, however, that about the
palace there were always some who would contrive to keep awake
at night, in order to be near her. But she soon began to take
every chance of getting away from her nurses and enjoying her
moonlight alone. And thus things went on until she was nearly
seventeen years of age.

As she grew older she had grown more and more beautiful,
with the sunniest hair and the loveliest eyes of heavenly blue,
brilliant and profound as the sky of a June day, but so much

more painful and sad was the change as her bad time came on. The more beautiful she was in the full moon, the more withered and worn did she become as the moon waned. At the time at which my story has now arrived, she looked, when the moon was small or gone, like an old woman exhausted with suffering.

A little way from the palace there was a great open glade, covered with the greenest and softest grass. This was her favourite haunt; for here the full moon shone free and glorious, while through the trees she could generally see more or less of the dying moon as it crossed the opening. Here she had a little rustic house built for her, and here she mostly resided. Whether the good fairies had anything to do with it or not, I cannot tell, but at last she got into the way of retreating farther into the wood every night as the moon waned, so that sometimes they had great trouble in finding her; but as she was always very angry if she discovered they were watching her, they scarcely dared to do so.

About this time, in a neighbouring kingdom, an insurrection took place upon the death of the old king, the greater part of the nobility was massacred, and the young prince was compelled to flee for his life, disguised like a peasant. For some time, until he got out of the country, he suffered much from hunger and fatigue; but when he got into that country ruled by the princess's father, and had no longer any fear of being recognized, he fared better, for the people were kind. He did not abandon his disguise, however.

For a day or two he had been walking through the palace wood, and had had next to nothing to eat, when he came upon the strangest little house, inhabited by a very nice, tidy, motherly old woman. This was one of the good fairies. The moment she saw him she knew quite well who he was, and what was going to come of it; but she was not at liberty to interfere with the orderly march of events. She received him with the kindness she would have shown to any other traveler, and gave him bread and milk, which he thought the most delicious food he had ever tasted, wondering that they did not have it for dinner at the palace sometimes.

The old woman pressed him to stay all night. When he awoke he was amazed to find how well and strong he felt. She would not take any of the money he offered but begged him, if he found occasion of continuing in the neighbourhood, to return and occupy the same quarters.

"Thank you much, good mother," answered the prince; "but there is little chance of that. The sooner I get out of this wood the better."

"I don't know that," said the fairy.

"What do you mean?" asked the prince.

"Why, how *should* I know?" returned she.

"I can't tell," said the prince.

"Very well," said the fairy.

"How strangely you talk!" said the prince.

"Do I?" said the fairy.

"Yes, you do," said the prince.

"Very well," said the fairy.

The prince was not used to be spoken to in this fashion, so he felt a little angry, and turned and walked away. But this did not offend the fairy. She stood at the door of her little house looking after him till the trees hid him quite. Then she said, "At last!" and went in.

The prince wandered and wandered, and got nowhere. The sun sank and sank, and went out of sight, and he seemed no nearer to the end of the wood than ever. He sat down on a fallen tree, ate a bit of bread the old woman had given him, and waited for the moon. Up she same, slow and slow, but of a good size, pretty round indeed; whereupon, greatly refreshed with his piece of bread, he got up and went—he knew not whither.

After walking a considerable distance, he thought he was coming to the outside of the forest; but when he reached what he thought the last of it he found himself only upon the edge of a great open space in it, covered with grass. The moon shone very bright, and he thought he had never seen a more lovely spot. Still, it looked dreary because of its loneliness, for he could not see the house at the other side. He sat down, weary again, and gazed into the glade. He had not seen so much room for several days.

All at once he spied something in the middle of the grass. What could it be? It moved; it came nearer. Was it a human creature, gliding across—a girl dressed in white, gleaming in the moonshine? She came nearer and nearer. He crept behind a tree and watched, wondering. It must be a nymph, he thought. But when she came close, he no longer doubted; she was human, for he caught sight of her sunny hair, and her clear blue eyes, and the loveliest face and form that he had ever seen.

All at once she began singing like a nightingale, and dancing to her own music, with her eyes ever turned toward the moon.

She passed close to where he stood, dancing on by the edge of the trees and away in a great circle toward the other side, until he could see but a spot of white in the yellowish green of the moonlit grass. But when he feared it would vanish quite, the spot grew, and became a figure once more. She approached him again, singing and dancing and waving her arms over her head, until she had completed the circle.

Just opposite his tree she stood, ceased her song, dropped her arms, and broke out into a long, clear laugh, musical as a brook. Then, as if tired, she threw herself on the grass, and lay gazing at the moon. The prince was almost afraid to breathe lest he should startle her, and she should vanish from his sight. As to venturing near her, that never came into his head.

Again she began dancing to her own music, and danced away into the distance. Once more she returned in a similar manner; but, although he was watching as eagerly as before, what with fatigue and what with gazing, he fell fast asleep before she came near him. When he awoke, it was broad daylight, and the princess was nowhere.

He could not leave the place. What if she should come the next night! He would gladly endure a day's hunger to see her yet again. He walked round the glade to see if he could discover any prints of her feet. But the grass was so short and her steps had been so light, that she had not left a single trace behind her.

He walked halfway round the wood without seeing anything to account for her presence. Then he spied a lovely little house, with thatched roof and low eaves, surrounded by an exquisite garden, with doves and peacocks walking in it. Of course this must be where the gracious lady who loved the moonlight lived.

Forgetting his appearance, he walked toward the door, determined to make inquiries; but as he passed a little pond full of gold and silver fishes, he caught sight of himself and turned to find the door to the kitchen. There he knocked, and asked for a piece of bread. The good-natured cook brought him in, and gave him an excellent breakfast, which the prince found nothing the worse for being served in the kitchen.

While he ate, he talked with his entertainer, and learned that this was the favourite retreat of the Princess Daylight. But he learned nothing more, both because he was afraid of seeming inquisitive, and because the cook did not choose to be heard talking about her mistress to a peasant lad who had begged for his breakfast.

As he rose to take his leave, it occurred to him that he might not be so far from the old woman's cottage as he had thought, and he asked the cook whether she knew anything of such a place, describing it as well as he could.

"Which way does it lie from here?" asked the prince.

She gave him full instructions; and he left her with many thanks.

Being now refreshed, however, the prince did not go back to the cottage that day; he remained in the forest, amusing himself as best he could, but waiting anxiously for the night, in the hope that the princess would again appear. Nor was he disappointed, for directly the moon rose he spied a glimmering shape far across the glade. As it drew nearer, he saw it was she, indeed—not dressed in white as before: in a pale blue like the sky, she looked lovelier still. He thought it was that the blue suited her yet better than the white; he did not know that she was really more beautiful because the moon was nearer the full. In fact, the next night was full moon, and the princess would then be at the zenith of her loveliness.

He watched the whole night long, and saw that as the moon went down she retreated in smaller and smaller circles, until at last he could see her no more.

Weary as he was, he set out for the old woman's cottage, where he arrived just in time for her breakfast, which she shared with him. He then went to bed, and slept for many hours. When he awoke the sun was down, and he departed in great anxiety lest he should lose a glimpse of the lovely vision. But he lost his way.

I shall not attempt to describe his misery when the moon rose, and he saw nothing but trees, trees, trees. She was high in the heaven before he reached the glade. Then, indeed, his trouble vanished, for there was the princess coming dancing toward him, in a dress that shone like gold, and with shoes that glimmered through the grass like fireflies. She was, of course, still more beautiful than before. Like an embodied sunbeam she passed him, and danced away into the distance.

Before she returned in her circle, clouds had begun to gather about the moon. The wind rose, the trees moaned, and their lighter branches leaned all one way before it. The prince feared that the princess would go in, and he should see her no more that night. But she came dancing on more jubilant than ever, her golden dress and her sunny hair streaming out upon the blast, waving her arms toward the moon. The prince could hardly believe she was not a creature of the elements, after all.

By the time she had completed another circle, the clouds had gathered deep, and there were growlings of distant thunder. Just as she passed the tree where he stood, a flash of lightning blinded him for a moment, and when he saw again, to his horror, the princess lay on the ground. He darted to her, thinking she had been struck; but when she heard him coming she was on her feet in a moment.

"What do you want?" she asked.

"I beg your pardon, I thought—the lightning——" said the prince, hesitating.

"There is nothing the matter," said the princess, waving him off rather haughtily.

The poor prince turned and walked toward the wood.

"Come back," said Daylight; "I like you. You do what you are told. Are you good?"

"Not so good as I should like to be," said the prince.

"Then go and grow better," said the princess.

Again the disappointed prince turned and went.

"Come back," said the princess.

He obeyed and stood before her, waiting.

"Can you tell me what the sun is like?" she asked.

"No," he answered. "But where's the good of asking what you know?"

"But I don't know," she rejoined.

"Why, everybody knows."

"That's the very thing; I'm not everybody. I've never seen the sun."

"Then you can't know what it's like till you do see it."

"I think you must be a prince," said the princess.

"Do I look like one?" said the prince.

"I can't quite say that."

"Then why do you think so?"

"Because you both do what you are told, and speak the truth. Is the sun so very bright?"

"As bright as the lightning."

"But it doesn't go out like that, does it?"

"Oh, no. It shines like the moon, rises and sets like the moon, is much the same shape as the moon, only so bright that you can't look at it for a moment."

"But *I would* look at it," said the princess.

"But you couldn't," said the prince.

"But I could," said the princess.

"Why don't you, then?"

"Because I can't."

"Why can't you?"

"Because I can't wake. And I never shall wake until——" Here she hid her face in her hands, turned away, and walked in the slowest, stateliest manner toward the house. The prince ventured to follow her at a little distance, but she turned and waved him back, and, like a true gentleman prince, he obeyed at once. He waited a long time, but as she did not come near him again, and as the night had now cleared, he set off at last for the old woman's cottage.

It was long past midnight when he reached it, but, to his surprise, the old woman was paring potatoes at the door. Fairies are fond of doing odd things. Indeed, however they may dissemble, the night is always their day. And so it is with all who have fairy blood in them.

"Why, what are you doing there, this time of the night, Mother?" said the prince; for that was the kind way in which any young man in his country would address a woman who was much older than himself.

"Getting your supper ready, my son," she answered.

"Oh! I don't want any supper," said the prince.

"Ah, you've seen Daylight!" said she.

"I've seen a princess who never saw it," said the prince.

"Do you like her?" asked the fairy.

"Oh, don't I?" said the prince. "More than you would believe, Mother."

"A fairy can believe anything that ever was or ever could be," said the old woman.

"Then you are a fairy?" asked the prince.

"Yes," said she.

"Then what do you do for things not to believe?" asked the prince.

"There's plenty of them—everything that never was nor ever could be."

"Plenty, I grant you," said the prince. "But do you believe there could be a princess who never saw the daylight? Do you believe that, now?"

This the prince said, not that he doubted the princess but that he wanted the fairy to tell him more. She was too old a fairy, however, to be caught so easily.

"Of all people, fairies must not tell secrets. Besides, she's a princess."

"Well, I'll tell *you* a secret. I'm a prince."

"I know that."

"How do you know it?"

"By the curl of the third eyelash on your left eyelid."

"Which corner do you count from?"

"That's a secret."

"Another secret? Well, at least, if I am a prince, there can be no harm in telling me about a princess."

"It's just princes I can't tell."

"There aren't any more of them—are there?"

"What! you don't think you're the only prince in the world, do you?"

"Oh, dear, no! not at all. But I know there's one too many just at present, except the princess——"

"Yes, yes, that's it," said the fairy.

"What's *it?*" asked the prince.

But he could get nothing more out of the fairy, and had to go to bed unanswered.

The prince had so far stolen a march upon the old witch that she did not know he was in the neighbourhood until after he had seen the princess those three times. Now, however, the witch was going to do all she could.

She so contrived it by her deceitful spells, that the next night the prince could not find his way to the glade. It would take me too long to tell her tricks. They would be amusing to us, who know that they could not do any harm, but they were something other than amusing to the poor prince. He wandered about the forest till daylight, and then fell fast asleep. The same thing occurred for seven following days, during which he could not find the good fairy's cottage.

After the third quarter of the moon, however, the bad fairy thought she might be at ease about the affairs for a fortnight at least, for there was no chance of the prince wishing to kiss the princess during that period. So the first day of the fourth quarter he did find the cottage, and the next day he found the glade. For nearly another week he haunted it. But the princess never came.

I have little doubt she was on the farther edge of it some part of every night, but at this period she always wore black, and there being little or no light, the prince never saw her. Nor would he have known her if he had seen her. How could he have taken the worn, decrepit creature she was now for the glorious Princess Daylight?

At last, one night when there was no moon at all, he ventured near the house. There he heard voices talking, although it was past midnight; for the women were in considerable uneasiness, because the one whose turn it was to watch the princess had fallen asleep, and had not seen which way she went. And this was a night when she would probably wander very far, describing a circle which did not touch the open glade at all, but stretched away from the back of the house, deep into that side of the forest —a part of which the prince knew nothing.

When he understood that the princess had disappeared, he plunged at once into the wood to see if he could find her. For hours he roamed with nothing to guide him but the vague notion of a circle, which on one side bordered on the house.

It was getting toward the dawn, but as yet there was no streak of light in the sky, when he came to a great birch tree, and sat down weary at the foot of it. While he sat very miserable, he bethought himself that it would not be a bad plan to light a fire, which, if the princess were anywhere near, would attract her. This he managed with a tinder box, which the good fairy had given him. It was just beginning to blaze up, when he heard a moan, which seemed to come from the other side of the tree.

He sprang to his feet, but his heart throbbed so that he had to lean for a moment against the tree before he could move. When he got round, there lay a human form in a little dark heap on the earth. There was light enough from his fire to show that it was not the princess. He lifted it in his arms, hardly heavier than a child, and carried it to the flame. The countenance was that of an old woman, but it had a fearfully strange look. A black hood concealed her hair, and her eyes were closed.

He laid her down as comfortably as he could, chafed her hands, put a little cordial from a bottle, also the gift of the fairy, into her mouth; took off his coat and wrapped it about her, in short, did the best he could. Soon she opened her eyes and looked at him—so pitifully!

The tears rose and flowed down her gray, wrinkled cheeks, but she said never a word. The tears kept on flowing, and her whole appearance was so utterly pitiful that the prince was very near crying, too. He begged her to tell him what was the matter, promising to do all he could to help her; but still she did not speak.

He thought she was dying, and took her in his arms again to carry her to the princess's house, where he thought the good-natured cook might be able to do something for her. When he lifted her, the tears flowed yet faster, and she gave a moan that went to his very heart.

"Mother, Mother!" he said, "poor Mother!" and kissed her on the withered lips.

She started; and what eyes they were that opened upon him! But he did not see them, for it was still very dark, and he had enough to do to make his way through the trees toward the house.

Just as he approached the door, feeling more tired than he could have imagined possible—she was such a little thin old thing —she began to move, and became so restless that, unable to carry her a moment longer, he thought to lay her on the grass. But she stood upright on her feet. Her hood had dropped, and her hair fell about her.

The first gleam of the morning was caught on her face: that face was bright as the never-aging Dawn, and her eyes were lovely as the sky of darkest blue. The prince recoiled in over-mastering wonder. It was Daylight herself whom he had brought from the forest! He fell at her feet, nor dared look up until she laid her hand upon his head. He rose then.

"You kissed me when I was an old woman; there! I kiss you when I am a young princess," murmured Daylight. "Is that the sun coming?"

THE HOUSE IN THE WOOD

A POOR woodman lived with his wife and three daughters in a little cottage on the edge of a lonesome wood. One morning as he was going out to work he said to his wife, "Wife, tell our eldest girl to bring my dinner after me to the wood, or I shall not get my work done; and that she may not lose her way, I will take with me a bag of oats, and strew them along the path."

When it was noon and the sun was high above the trees, the little girl set out with a jug-full of soup. But the sparrows, the larks, finches, blackbirds, and thrushes had picked up all the oats and the maiden could not find the path. So she wandered on at random, until the sun went down and night closed in. The trees rustled in the darkness, the owls screeched, and she began to be afraid. As the maiden was going along, all at once she saw in the distance a light glimmering among the trees.

"Over there must surely be some dwelling," she thought and she hastened toward the spot.

It was not long before she came to a house, in the window of which was a light. She tapped at the door, and a rough voice from within cried, "Come in!" When the little girl opened the door she saw a gray-haired old man sitting at a table. His head rested upon his two hands, and his white beard hung down nearly to the ground. On the hearth there lay a little cock, a hen, and

197

a brindled cow. Then the little girl told the man that she had lost her way and begged him to let her rest there for the night; whereupon the old man turned to the hearth and said:

> "My pretty cock,
> My pretty hen,
> And you, my brindled cow,
> Tell me, all, what think you now?"

"Let her stay," they all cried at once. Then the old man, turning to the little girl, said, "In the kitchen you will find plenty of everything to eat and drink. Go and cook us a supper."

She went into the kitchen and cooked a good supper, but she did not once think of the animals on the hearth. When all was ready she took the dish, placed it on the table before the old man, and then sat down and satisfied her hunger. And when she had eaten as much as she liked, she said, "I am tired. Where is my bed, and where shall I sleep?"

But the animals by the fire answered:

> "You have had food, and you have had drink,
> But of us you had not the grace to think;
> So find as you can for yourself a bed,
> For what care we where you lay your head."

Then the old man said to the girl: "Go upstairs, child, and you will find two rooms with a bed in each. The first room is mine. Go into it, shake the bed, cover it with white linen, and put the pillows in their places. I shall come to bed presently. When you have done this you may go into the next room. There you will find your own bed."

So the little girl went upstairs as she was bidden, and when she had shaken the first bed and spread it neatly, she laid herself down on it and fell asleep. After a while, up came the gray-haired old man. When he saw the little girl fast asleep in his bed, he held the candle close to the maiden's face, looked at her, shook his head, and looked very sad. Then he opened a trap door and let her gently down into the cellar.

Late in the evening the woodman returned home and chid his wife for letting him go all day without food. "I am not to blame," she answered. "I sent the girl with your dinner, as you wished; she has perhaps lost her way, but no doubt she will soon come back."

The next morning the woodman got up before daybreak and when he went to work he told his wife to send their second daughter with his dinner. "This time," said he, "I will take a bag of peas with me. They are bigger than oats, so the child will see them better and cannot lose her way."

At noon the little girl set out for the wood, with a basketful of food upon her arm. But when she came there, the peas, alas! had all vanished; for the birds had picked them up, as they did the oats, and not one was left. So the child wandered about for a long time in the wood, and when it grew dark she, too, came to the house of the old man, and begged for food and lodging. Thereupon the old man with the white beard again turned to his animals, and said:

THE HOUSE IN THE WOOD

"My pretty cock,
My pretty hen,
    And you, my pretty brindled cow,
Tell me, I pray, what think you now?"

"Let her stay," answered the animals. And it all happened with the second girl as it did with the first. She cooked a good supper, ate and drank with the old man, but never troubled her head about the animals. When she asked where she could sleep they answered:

"You have had food and you have had drink,
    But of us you had not the grace to think,
    So find as you can for yourself a bed,
    For what care we where you lay your head."

The child soon afterwards went upstairs to make the beds and when she had fallen asleep, the old man came, looked at her with a shake of his head, and let her and the bed down into the cellar.

The third morning when the woodman got up he said to his wife, "Wife, send our youngest child with my dinner to-day. She has always been good and obedient and will keep to the right path, and not go roving about like her sisters." But the tears came into the good woman's eyes as she said, "Must I lose my dearest child, too?"

"Do not trouble yourself, wife," answered he. "The girl is too clever and sensible to lose her way. But to make all sure, I will take some beans with me. They are bigger than peas and will show her the path clearly enough."

At dinner time, therefore, the little girl went her way to the wood, with the basket on her arm; but lo and behold! the wood-pigeons had already filled their crops with the beans and she did not know which way to turn. Then she was in great trouble, every minute thinking how hungry her poor father would be and how her good mother would cry and grieve if she did not come home. At length when it was dark, she spied a light through the trees and, following this, she came to the old man's house. In a sweet and gentle voice she begged leave to stay there for the night and the old man with the white beard asked his animals as before:

> "My pretty cock,
> My pretty hen,
> And you, my pretty brindled cow,
> Tell me, all, what think you now?"

"Let her stay," they cried, one and all. Then the child stepped to the hearth where the animals lay, fondled the little cock and hen, stroked their smooth feathers, and gently scratched the brindled cow between her horns. And when at the bidding of the old man, she had got ready a good supper, and the dish was standing upon the table, the little girl said to herself, "Shall I eat and drink and those poor animals have nothing? There is plenty of food out of doors and I will first care for them."

Then she went into the yard, fetched some oatmeal and

strewed it before the cock and hen, and brought the cow a whole apronful of sweet-smelling hay.

"Eat and enjoy it, you dear creatures," said she, "and if you are thirsty I will bring you a draught of fresh water." So saying, away she tripped, and presently fetched a pailful of water. The cock and hen hopped upon the rim of the pail, dipped their beaks into the water, and then turned up their heads as birds do when they drink; and the brindled cow took a good hearty draught.

When the animals were fed, but not till then, the little girl sat down at the table by the old man, and ate her supper. In a little while the cock and hen nestled their heads under their wings, and the brindled cow's eyes blinked. Then said the maiden, "Shall we not go to rest?" So the old man again said:

> "Pretty little cock,
> Pretty little hen,
> And you, my pretty brindled cow,
> Tell me, all, what think you now?"

"Let her stay," answered the animals, and turning to the little girl they said:

> "You have had food and you have had drink,
> And kindly of us you were pleased to think;
> And so, pretty maiden, we wish you good-night,
> May your pillow be soft and your dreams be light!"

Then the maiden went upstairs, shook up the old man's bed, put clean sheets upon it, and put the pillows in their places. When she had finished she called to the old man and told him that his bed was ready, and she wished him a good-night.

Then she went into her own room and closed the door.

She slept soundly till midnight, when suddenly there arose such a disturbance in the house that she awoke. In every corner there was a rattling and clattering. The doors flew open and slammed against the walls, and the rafters creaked and creaked as if they were wrenched out of their joints; the staircase, too, seemed to be coming down with a crash, and the whole roof to be tumbling about their ears. But soon again all was quiet; and the little girl again fell asleep.

In the morning the sun shone brightly in at the window and awakened her; but what do you think she beheld? She was lying in a large and splendid room, and everything around her shone and glittered as if she were in a king's palace. On the walls were golden flowers embroidered upon a green silk ground; the bed was of carved ivory; the counterpane of crimson velvet and on a chair by the bedside stood a pair of slippers embroidered with pearls. The little girl thought it was all a dream, but presently in came three servants in splendid dresses, and asked what commands she would be pleased to give.

"Leave me," said the little girl. "I will get up at once and cook some breakfast for the old man, and then I will feed the cock and hen and the brindled cow."

One of the servants brought beautiful dresses for the little girl and soon the child was dressed like a princess.

THE HOUSE IN THE WOOD

She thought the old man was already up; but she was no sooner dressed than she heard a gentle tap upon her door and the old man entered. As the child looked at him a great change took place. To her surprise and amazement the old man became a young and handsome prince standing before her.

"I am a king's son," he said. "I have been obliged by a wicked spell to live in the woods in the form of an old man. The spell could not be broken until a gentle child should come who would be as kind-hearted toward my animals as to me. You are that maiden and at midnight the spell was broken. I am myself again and my animals, too, are free. My little house in the woods is changed into my royal palace."

Then the king's son commanded his three servants to ride off and fetch the maiden's father and mother.

"But where are my two sisters?" she asked.

"Your sisters are shut up safely in my cellar," answered the prince.

"To-morrow I shall order them to be taken into the wood where they shall be servants to the charcoal-burners until they have learned to be gentle and kind to all animals and not let them go without food or drink."

JORINDA AND JORINDEL

THERE was once an old castle that stood in the middle of a large thick wood, and in the castle lived an old fairy. All the day long she flew about in the form of an owl, or crept about the country like a cat; but at night she always became an old woman again. When any youth came within a hundred paces of her castle, he became quite fixed, and could not move a step till she came and set him free: but when any pretty maiden came within that distance, she was changed into a bird; and the fairy put her into a cage and hung her up in a chamber in the castle. There were seven hundred of these cages hanging in the castle, and all with beautiful birds in them.

Now there was once a maiden whose name was Jorinda: she was prettier than all the pretty girls that ever were seen; and a shepherd whose name was Jorindel was very fond of her, and they were soon to be married. One day they went to walk in the wood, that they might be alone; and Jorindel said, "We must take care that we don't go too near to the castle." It was a beautiful evening; the last rays of the setting sun shone bright through the long stems of the trees upon the green underwood beneath, and the turtledoves sang plaintively from the tall birches.

Jorinda sat down to gaze upon the sun; Jorindel sat by her side; and both felt sad, they knew not why; but it seemed as if they were to be parted from one another for ever. They had wandered a long way; and when they looked to see which way they should go home, they found themselves at a loss to know what path to take.

The sun was setting fast, and already half of his circle had disappeared behind the hill: Jorindel on a sudden looked behind him, and as he saw through the bushes that they had, without knowing it, sat down close under the old walls of the castle, he shrank for fear, turned pale, and trembled. Jorinda was singing,

> The ring-dove sang from the willow spray,
>> Well-a-day! well-a-day!
> He mourn'd for the fate
> Of his lovely mate,
>> Well-a-day!

The song ceased suddenly. Jorindel turned to see the reason, and beheld his Jorinda changed into a nightingale; so that her song ended with a mournful *jug, jug*. An owl with fiery eyes flew three times round them, and three times screamed Tu whu! Tu whu! Tu whu! Jorindel could not move: he stood fixed as a stone, and could neither weep, nor speak, nor stir hand or foot. And now the sun went quite down; the gloomy night came; the owl flew into a bush; and a moment after the old fairy came forth pale and meagre, with staring eyes, and a nose and chin that almost met one another.

She mumbled something to herself, seized the nightingale, and went away with it in her hand. Poor Jorindel saw the nightingale was gone,—but what could he do? He could not speak, he could not move from the spot where he stood. At last the fairy came back, and sung with a hoarse voice,

> Till the prisoner's fast,
> And her doom is cast,
>   There stay! Oh, stay!
> When the charm is around her,
> And the spell had bound her,
>   Hie away! away!

On a sudden Jorindel found himself free. Then he fell on his knees before the fairy, and prayed her to give him back his dear Jorinda: but she said he should never see her again, and went her way.

He prayed, he wept, he sorrowed, but all in vain. "Alas!" he said, "what will become of me?"

He could not return to his own home, so he went to a strange village, and employed himself in keeping sheep. Many a time did he walk round and round as near to the hated castle as he dared go. At last he dreamt one night that he found a beautiful purple flower, and in the middle of it lay a costly pearl; and he dreamt that he plucked the flower, and went with it in his hand into the castle, and that everything he touched with it was disenchanted, and that there he found his dear Jorinda again.

In the morning when he awoke, he began to search over hill and dale for this pretty flower; and eight long days he sought for it in vain: but on the ninth day early in the morning he found the beautiful purple flower; and in the middle of it was a large dew drop as big as a costly pearl.

Then he plucked the flower, and set out and travelled day and night till he came again to the castle. He walked nearer than a hundred paces to it, and yet he did not become fixed as before, but found that he could go close up to the door.

Jorindel was very glad to see this: he touched the door with the flower, and it sprang open, so that he went in through the court, and listened when he heard so many birds singing. At last he came to the chamber where the fairy sat, with the seven hundred birds singing in the seven hundred cages. And when she saw Jorindel she was very angry, and screamed with rage; but she could not come within two yards of him; for the flower he held in his hand protected him. He looked around at the birds, but alas! there were many many nightingales, and how then should he find his Jorinda? While he was thinking what to do, he observed that the fairy had taken down one of the cages, and was making her escape through the door. He ran or flew to her, touched the cage with the flower,—and his Jorinda stood before him. She threw her arms round his neck and looked as beautiful as ever, as beautiful as when they walked together in the wood.

Then he touched all the other birds with the flower, so that they resumed their old forms; and took his dear Jorinda home, where they lived happily together many years.